ZOM-B
GODDESS

'Zom-B Goddess doesn't disappoint. We get another huge twist, another big moment for B to shine and a suitably mind-blowing ending to a series that has made me gasp in shock at least once per book.' So Many Books, So Little Time

'This last instalment of Darren Shan's zombie series is epic. It's as full of graphic gore as you could wish, has a plot twist on every other page, and includes the biggest battle of the sequence yet.' The Bookbag

'It's been a ride worthy of an apocalypse, and Mr Darren Shan has given us another crazy collection of novels that inspire and intrigue' Bookblog Bonanza

'Wow. I did NOT see that ending coming. Even down to the wire, Shan's got tons of surprises up his sleeve, and he deploys them by the megaton.' Reader, Writer, Fanboy

DARREN SHAN
ZOM-B
GODDESS

SIMON & SCHUSTER

ALSO BY DARREN SHAN

ZOM-B

First published in Great Britain in 2016 by Simon and Schuster UK Ltd
This edition published 2017
A CBS COMPANY

1 3 5 7 9 10 8 6 4 2

Simon & Schuster UK Ltd
1st Floor
222 Gray's Inn Road
London WC1X 8HB

Simon & Schuster Australia, Sydney
Simon & Schuster India, New Delhi

A CIP catalogue record for this book
is available from the British Library.

HB ISBN: 978-0-85707-796-7
PB ISBN: 978-0-85707-798-1
EBOOK ISBN: 978-0-85707-799-8

This book is a work of fiction. Names, characters, places and
incidents are either the product of the author's imagination or are
used fictitiously. Any resemblance to actual people living or
dead, events or locales is entirely coincidental.

Printed and bound by CPI Group (UK) Ltd, Croydon, CR0 4YY

www.simonandschuster.co.uk
www.simonandschuster.com.au

MIX
Paper from
responsible sources
FSC® C020471

Simon & Schuster UK Ltd are committed to sourcing paper
that is made from wood grown in sustainable forests and support the Forest
Stewardship Council, the leading international forest certification organisation.
Our books displaying the FSC logo are printed on FSC certified paper.

THEN . . .

Humanity's control of the world ended one blood-soaked day when the dead came back to life and ran wild across the globe. Society collapsed in the space of a few short, shocking hours, and nothing would ever be the same again.

Becky Smith was one of the casualties. Even though her heart was ripped from her chest, she'd been infected by one of the undead, so became a brain-munching zombie. Months later she recovered her senses and took her first tentative steps as a monster with a conscience.

B learnt, as time moved on, that a war was being fought to determine the fate of the planet. Two powerful forces were pitted against one another on the streets of London. An insane clown, Mr Dowling, stood on one side with an army of mutants and savage babies. The kindly Dr Oystein stood on the other, with his team of compassionate, revitalised, zombie Angels.

Dr Oystein told B that two viruses existed. One, Clements-13, would wipe out every zombie in existence within a couple of weeks if it was released. The other, Schlesinger-10, would kill off all of the surviving humans just as swiftly. The doctor possessed a sample of the crimson, zombie-destroying Clements-13, but Mr Dowling had got his hands on a vial of the milky-white, human-annihilating Schlesinger-10, forcing a stand-off.

Having suffered more than most of her wretched kind, B eventually wound up in the clutches of the murderous clown, held captive in his underground lair. He professed his love for her, and she eventually agreed to marry him in exchange for his vow to stop killing. On their wedding night, reacting to some hidden command buried deep inside her head, she mentally ripped the location of his vial of Schlesinger-10 from his thoughts. Mr Dowling attacked her and they fought like tigers. B managed to escape with the aid of a cloned baby whom she had nick-named Holy Moly.

Storing the vial in the cavity of her stomach (which had been carved open and largely emptied of intestines and internal organs), B headed for the sur-face, desperate to pass it on to Dr Oystein, so that he could deploy his mixture of Clements-13 without fear of retaliation.

While waiting for the doctor in an old brewery, B found evidence that she had been played for a sap. She was horrified to discover that it was Dr Oystein who had masterminded the release of the zombie virus which had brought the world crashing to its knees. Shocked and furious, she struck out at the man she had grown to love and respect, then fled, terrified of what he would do if he had both vials in his possession.

All seemed lost when some of B's fellow Angels trapped her, but she was rescued by an ex-soldier, Barnes. He took her to a safe house and the pair planned their departure from London. But, late that night, a familiar foe of B's appeared — Owl Man, so called because of his massive eyes. Owl Man had a sinister psychic hold over B, and to her horror he ordered her to kill Barnes. A slave to his whims, she automatically obeyed.

As B stared sickly at her dead comrade, Owl Man pointed to the doorway and Dr Oystein calmly entered the old pub where she and Barnes had based themselves. Taking a seat, the doctor told B that Owl Man was his nephew, and that he and she needed to have a little talk ...

NOW . . .

ONE

Dr Oystein stares at me solemnly as I glare at him and try to break the spell that I'm under. But, as much as I strain and twitch, my limbs won't do what I want. Owl Man is in command of my body and I can't move until he frees me.

'There is such ferocity in her expression,' Owl Man murmurs, running his fingers over his bulging stomach and pursing his lips. 'I think she would rip your head off if I released her.'

'No,' Dr Oystein says softly. 'She could have killed

me in the brewery if she wished to end my life. I was at her mercy but she spared me.'

'That was a mistake,' I snarl, hating myself for what I've done to Barnes, hating Dr Oystein and Owl Man for making me do it. 'If the chance comes my way again ...'

Dr Oystein sighs. He studies me sadly for a few seconds, then stands and fetches another seat. He positions it behind me and nods at Owl Man.

'You may sit, Becky,' Owl Man says, and I slide backwards on to the chair.

Dr Oystein sits opposite me, hands resting on his knees. He looks tired, bloody and bruised from our fight earlier. Owl Man stands just behind him. Sakarias pads across, lies by its master's feet and closes its eyes. It looks like an ordinary sheepdog now, no sign of mutant claws or fangs.

There's movement behind me. Rage enters by the back door, grinning wickedly. He must have rowed ashore and tied Barnes's boat back up at the pier. He spots the corpse and laughs harshly.

'I bet Owl Man made you kill him,' Rage chuckles.

'You'll be next,' I promise.

'Not as long as I'm a loyal servant,' he says, taking his place by Owl Man's side, every bit as faithful as the snoozing dog on the floor.

'Let me at him,' I plead.

'No,' Owl Man says. 'Besides, in your current condition, it would not be a fair contest.'

'That is why she asked you to let her fight,' Dr Oystein says. 'She wants him to destroy her brain, so that she can escape. I do not blame her. After all that she has suffered, she deserves the relief of true death.'

'Fine words,' I sneer. 'Back them up with action if you mean them.'

'I will,' he says, to my surprise. 'When we are done here, if you wish for me to execute you, I'll do that great and terrible thing. You have served my cause in ways no one else ever has, and I know you have paid a dreadful price. If oblivion is the reward you crave, I'll grant it.

'Release her, Zachary,' Dr Oystein says, calling Owl Man by his preferred title, even though the creep's real name is Tom White.

Owl Man looks uncertain. 'Are you sure that's wise?'

'I think that she is ready to listen to us now,' Dr Oystein says. 'If not, you can always reassert your authority over her.'

'Very well.' Owl Man waves a hand at me. 'You're free,' he says, and I feel myself relaxing back to normal. As soon as my limbs are my own, I hurl myself at Dr Oystein, fingers clawing for his eyes.

'Stop!' Owl Man barks, and I freeze. 'Sit,' he says, and I return to my chair.

'It seems that you were right and I was wrong, Zachary,' the doc notes glumly.

'Sorry,' I mutter. 'It was a knee-jerk reaction. Let me go. I won't do it again. I promise.'

Owl Man cocks an eyebrow at Dr Oystein. The doc doesn't hesitate, nodding immediately. 'Very well,' Owl Man says. 'You're free again, Becky.'

I'm out of my chair even before he's finished saying my name, and this time I almost get my hands on an unflinching Dr Oystein before Owl Man exerts his control over me and once more sends me back to the chair.

'It's hopeless, Oystein,' he says. 'The girl is beyond reason.'

'So it seems,' the doc murmurs. 'Yet I would try with her, Zachary, again and again. She is worth so much more than you or I, and I hate what we have done to her.' He grimaces. 'But we don't have all night. I will leave her a prisoner of your wishes for the time being.'

'Ever the gent,' I sneer, then glare at Own Man. I hate this tall man in the striped suit, with his pot belly and abnormally large eyes, but I'm impressed at the same time. 'How the hell do you do this anyway? The doc said you hypnotised me when I was a kid. Is that true?'

'I certainly hypnotised you,' Owl Man purrs, 'but more recently than that. I did it when you returned from your first encounter with one of Albrecht's babies, after it had killed your artist friend.'

I think back. 'You mean when I was in the Groove Tube?' That was a long time ago. I was in bad shape then – though nowhere near as bad as I am now – and had to spend a few weeks immersed in the restorative liquid, in a blissed-out, uncon-scious state.

'I couldn't hypnotise you while you were in a state of suspension,' Owl Man says, 'but I did it not long afterwards. When you were fished out and told Dr Oystein what had happened with the baby, he could see that you were a crucial player in his war with Mr Dowling. He asked me if I would establish a control mechanism, so that we could steady you if we thought that you were going astray. He led you out of County Hall and brought you to me, so that I could work my charms on you. At the end of our many sessions together, I told you to wipe the memory of our encounter from your thoughts. That is why you have no recollection of it.'

'So you were in league with Owl Man even then,' I spit at the doc.

'Of course,' he says glumly. 'As I told you, Zachary is my nephew. We have had our differences over the years, and it was important that certain individuals believed we were still on confrontational terms, but we have been cooperating closely for a long time now, as you will have seen in the records that you found in the brewery.'

'They made for cheery reading, didn't they?' Rage snorts.

'You read them too?' I frown.

'Sure,' he says. 'I went there the night that we got back from New Kirkham, while the rest of you were guarding Dan-Dan in the suburbs. I had a feeling there was more to what happened with your old teacher, Billy Burke, than met the eye.'

I remember that night, Rage sneaking out, looking ashen when he returned, sitting apart from the rest of us, brooding. A conversation we had in Battersea comes back to me. He told me to make for Brick Lane to look for answers. I'd forgotten all about that, at least on a conscious level.

'That's when I decided to switch sides,' Rage goes on. 'The doc had tricked me, made me think there might be truly decent people out there, that they had a chance of changing the world for the better. I started to think that I could be a hero. But then I saw he was a liar. To be honest, I was relieved when I found out that the doc was as twisted as the rest of us. It freed me to go back to the way I was.'

Dr Oystein says nothing to defend himself while Rage is criticising him. I find myself getting hot under the collar. I want to tell Rage to shut up, that he's got no right to criticise a man of Dr Oystein's calibre. Then I think about what I learnt earlier tonight. I remind myself that, even though I don't want to believe it, and as much as it pains me to admit it, my beloved mentor is a villain beyond compare. And I keep my mouth closed.

'We have so much to discuss,' the doc says. 'This is a night for revelations. I have told you many lies in the past, or subtly distorted things that were true. No more. I will be honest with you in this final stretch. All that I can share, I will. But first I must know about the vial. Zachary?' He glances back at Owl Man. 'It is vital that she answers honestly.'

'Becky,' Owl Man says. 'Tell us the truth.'

I feel my jaw tighten, my tongue no longer quite my own.

Dr Oystein leans forward tensely. 'Did you discover where Mr Dowling was storing his vial of Schlesinger-10?'

I want to lie, to prevent him finding out what has happened to the virus that could wipe out the whole of humanity if released, but I can't. 'Yes,' I groan.

'Did you go in pursuit of it?' Dr Oystein presses.

Again I'm forced to answer truthfully. 'Yes.'

'And did you take it?' he hisses.

'Yes,' I grunt. 'I wedged it into my stomach and fled with it inside me.'

The doc's eyes sparkle as brightly as the undead's ever can. He lurches forward as if to rip through the bandages which Barnes wrapped round me. Then he stops himself and sits back, smiling warmly.

'No. That can wait. We are relatively safe here. We have some time to play with. Let us talk first. Then we will attend to other matters.'

The doc licks his lips, looks at the bandages again, then strokes his chin and casts his thoughts back.

'Where to begin?' he muses aloud. 'We cannot go

down every trail – my full story would require weeks to tell – but I will try to cover the key points as swiftly as I can. I suppose I should commence with a tale that I partly shared with you before, about when I was a prisoner of the Nazis . . .'

TWO

The doc had told me a while back that he and his brother had been forced by the Nazis to try to create zombies. They'd been imprisoned with a team of other brilliant scientists and told to find a way for their captors to cheat death.

'I neglected to tell you that my brother, Albrecht, would later become Mr Dowling,' Dr Oystein says, 'but most of the rest was true. The pair of us cracked the zombie gene and created the first reviveds. Then, when we learnt that our families were no longer being safeguarded, we tried to escape. We were caught and, as punishment, infected with the deadly seed of our creation.'

What the doc didn't tell me then, but admits now, was that he and his brother had also secretly come up with the formula for the revitalising vaccine that could bring some brain-munchers back to their senses.

'We knew we could never give that to the Nazis,' he says hollowly. 'With that power, the war and the world would have been theirs. The Nazis were creatures of pure malevolence, and we refused to subject humanity to their horrific rule. Even under torture we gave nothing away.'

The brothers had feared capture, and had guessed that they might be injected with the undead gene if caught. In a bid to counter that, each injected himself with a sample of the revitalising vaccine before they made their break for freedom.

'So you were telling porkies about God restoring your mind,' Rage sniggers.

'No,' Dr Oystein says stiffly. 'God *did* intercede. The odds against anyone revitalising are astronomical. For both of us to recover . . . it had to be a miracle.'

Miracle my arse! The doc might still see the hand of God in all this, but I know better. It was just a fluke, one of those random twists of fate that the universe throws up every now and then. But I don't bother arguing the point. It would be a waste of time. You can't reason with a madman.

The doc tells me that Albrecht recovered first, but waited for Oystein, acting for several weeks as if he was still one of the mindless reviveds. When his brother revitalised, the pair freed the other zombies from their cages, unleashed them on the Nazis, then destroyed all the records that they could find, before terminating the undead and burning their corpses, leaving no trace of their operation behind.

That should have been the start of a bright new chapter for the victorious brothers, but the doc just couldn't let the dead lie. In his unhinged state, he was convinced that God had tasked him with starting a zombie plague. As far as he was concerned, mankind had sinned gravely and needed to be punished severely. He devoted himself to improving the virus that they'd concocted, mastering its every nuance, so that he could one day wreak havoc with it.

Albrecht wasn't aware of his brother's twisted plans. He wanted to halt the spread of the virus. They knew that samples had been sent to other scientists, and he was worried that one of them would create an undead army. He worked with Oystein to learn more about the walking dead, but he thought their goal was to use that information to help humankind.

'So Mr Dowling was the good guy,' I mutter, barely able to believe it.

'I hope that *I* am doing good,' Dr Oystein demurs, and I choke back a sickened snort. 'But yes, Albrecht walked a less deceptive path than I did.'

Dr Oystein was keen to release the virus after the end of the war, but didn't feel ready. He longed to wipe out the living – since he thought they were mostly evil or weak – but he didn't want to immediately eliminate all conscious beings. Revitaliseds could live for a few thousand years, but then they'd die out, with no one to replace them. Craving a legacy, he continued to experiment, and then Albrecht, who had been working on creating an army of mutants – the idea being that they could act as warriors in the war with the living dead – came up with the idea for the babies.

'I knew that the babies were the future,' Dr Oystein says passionately. 'Albrecht only wished to use them to battle the reviveds, but I saw that they could serve a higher purpose, and ultimately take the place of the living.'

While Albrecht focused on developing different kinds of mutants, Oystein spent a lot of time trying to perfect the revitalising vaccine, so that he could start building a team of Angels to help him reshape the future world of his dreams.

'The vaccine continued to be unstable,' he says. 'I managed to enhance its child-orientated properties, but that was as far as I got.'

'Why focus on children?' I ask.

The doc smiles. 'They're less set in their ways than adults. I couldn't win the war alone. I had Albrecht, of course, and a few other trusty assistants, but they were not enough. I needed to put together a small, committed force to help me steer a course through the difficult centuries ahead of us. My fear was that adults would repeat the mistakes of the past, whereas children would be innocents that I could mould and shape.'

Dr Oystein also worked hard to develop a virus which would eliminate every last living survivor, but leave the undead and mutants intact.

'Perversely, I had an easy time developing the opposite of what I was after.' He chuckles wryly. 'For once I got the jump on my brother. While he struggled to make a virus that would destroy all zombies, I cracked that formula quite quickly.'

'So you lied about creating the human virus first?'

'Yes. Initially I produced a pure, virulent sample of the zombie-killing virus.' He sighs. 'Unfortunately that led to a savage row with Albrecht when he ...'

The doc stops. Owl Man's dog, Sakarias, has risen suddenly and is facing the door, growling softly. As Dr Oystein's head turns, I open my mouth to roar, hoping to create a disturbance that I can take advantage of. But, before I can scream, Owl Man hisses, 'Be quiet.' And my lips are sealed.

We stare at the door. There are footsteps outside, drawing nearer. Owl Man and Rage step up beside Dr Oystein, who has got to his feet. They weren't expecting this. If it's bad news for them, surely it can only be good news for me. Or so I tell myself.

'Probably just zombies,' Rage whispers.

Owl Man shakes his head. 'Sakarias does not react to the undead.'

'Angels?' Rage guesses.

This time it's Dr Oystein who shakes his head. 'I dismissed all of my people from the area before I summoned Zachary to help me find B.'

'Maybe it's Santa Claus,' Rage jokes, but uncle and nephew are in no mood for levity. I expect them to produce weapons, but they just stand there, staring, Owl Man gently squeezing the back of Sakarias's neck to stop the dog growling.

The footsteps come nearer . . . nearer . . . and stop just outside. Dr Oystein didn't close the door when

he entered — a schoolboy error, though I suppose he didn't think he had anything to fear. Whoever's out there can see the light shining within. There's a pause and hushed muttering, then the door's pushed open and three people are revealed on the pavement, and they're neither living nor undead — they're a few of Mr Dowling's mutants.

THREE

The mutants bear the marks of all of their kind. Ruined, purplish, pustulent flesh, strips of it peeling away in places. Grey hair, yellow eyes, blackened teeth, with gaps in their gums where some have fallen out. Two of them are men. The other is a girl, maybe a couple of years older than me.

They seem as shocked by our appearance as we are by theirs. I don't know what they were expecting to find – maybe they were searching for me – but I doubt they ever dreamt of stumbling upon their arch-enemy, Dr Oystein.

The mutants gawp at us, blinking dumbly. Then, before they can recover their senses, Owl Man says to Sakarias, 'Attack.'

The sheepdog bounds forward with a howl of vicious pleasure, baring its fangs, claws extending from its paws. I've seen the dog in action before. It's a dangerous opponent if you know what to anticipate, but even deadlier if it catches you unawares. The mutants weren't expecting the fangs and claws. They're not sure what to make of the animal barrelling towards them. And those few seconds of confusion damn them to defeat before the battle has properly started.

Sakarias leaps at the nearest mutant – one of the men – and drives him to the ground. As he lands with a startled cry, the dog whips its right paw across his throat. The claws tear the mutant's throat to ribbons and blood spurts into the air.

Sakarias doesn't wait around to wallow in the gushing blood. Instead, as the second man scrabbles for a weapon, the dog hurls itself into the air again, and this time strikes with its fangs. It clamps them round the man's face and crushes it, and the mutant's screams as his cheeks implode are terrible and piercing.

The girl turns to flee, but Owl Man calls to her. 'If you try to run, you'll die.'

She looks back, eyes wide with fear. Sakarias finishes with the second man – the first is still thrashing, but will soon be as dead as the one who is now missing a face – and its back legs tense as it prepares to spring again.

'Hold, old friend,' Owl Man says, and the dog relaxes immediately, though it doesn't retract its fangs or claws.

The girl blinks at the dog, then at Owl Man.

'I've seen you before,' Owl Man says, stepping up to the doorway and looking left and right outside. 'It's Claudia, isn't it?'

The girl gulps and nods. 'I've seen you too,' she says. 'You were at the wedding.'

Owl Man sighs. 'That was one of my happier recent days. What a shame the honeymoon had to end like this.' He steps back inside and beckons her forward. She blanches but obeys, veering round Sakarias, who is still on the pavement, studying her intently, waiting for the order to pounce.

'What are you doing here?' Owl Man asks the girl, now standing just inside the entrance, trembling uncontrollably.

'Searching for her,' Claudia says, nodding at me. 'Teams of us have been looking all over London for that cow. She assaulted our leader. Tried to kill him. We want her back so she can answer for her crimes.'

I try to respond to that, but I can't say anything. Owl Man hasn't given me clearance to speak yet.

'We saw some Angels on the prowl in this area earlier,' Claudia continues. 'We reported back. Mr Dowling is busy in County Hall, hunting for *you*,' she says, pointing to Dr Oystein. 'He thinks you're still in there. He's been tearing the place apart, looking for secret hidey-holes.'

'He will have a long and fruitless search,' Dr Oystein says with satisfaction.

'He killed all the Angels you left behind,' Claudia jeers.

The doc stiffens, then sighs. 'That is no surprise to me. What did your master say when you reported seeing Angels in the East End?'

'Nothing,' she smirks. 'He's not one for words. But Kinslow told us to stick around and see what they were up to. When they pulled out, we called in again. He said to give the area a quick once-over, but didn't seem to think too much of it. If he'd had any idea that *you* were here . . .' She points to Dr Oystein again.

'So you're on your own,' Owl Man notes.

'I am now,' Claudia says. With an effort, she stops herself trembling. 'So you might as well go ahead and kill me if you can, but don't think I'll make it easy for you. I don't have fangs like your dog, but I pack a mean old bite all the same.'

'I'm sure you do,' Owl Man smiles. Then the smile fades and he thinks about it for a few seconds. 'I'd rather not put you to the test, Claudia.'

'Zachary . . .' Dr Oystein murmurs.

'No,' Owl Man replies. 'There has been enough bloodshed. I know there must be more before this is through, but let's not kill those we can afford to spare. You and I are monsters, but we have to draw the line somewhere. Let's draw it here.'

Dr Oystein looks troubled, but he nods reluctantly.

Owl Man turns to the girl again. 'Leave your walkie-talkie,' he says. 'Return to County Hall. Tell Mr Dowling that you found me with Becky Smith and Dr Oystein.'

'Don't forget to mention me too,' Rage quips, but everyone ignores him.

'Tell him it's over,' Owl Man continues. 'The outcome has been decided, since we have Becky Smith and what she stole from him. Ask him to return to his base. I'll come to meet with him later, to discuss the future and accept my execution at his hands if he wishes to punish me for siding with his most bitter enemy.'

'You think he'll believe that?' Claudia snorts.

Owl Man shrugs. 'I've already won, so why would I lie?'

Claudia chews at her lip uncertainly.

'The alternative is taking your chances with Sakarias,' Owl Man murmurs, and she trembles again when the dog growls at the mention of its name.

'Here,' she spits, throwing a walkie-talkie to the floor. 'And I hope you all rot in Hell for what you've done.'

With that, she steps outside, gives Sakarias the evil eye, spares a sad glance for her fallen colleagues, then takes off into the night without looking back.

FOUR

'You have a soft heart, nephew,' Dr Oystein whispers.

Rage snorts but says nothing. I have plenty to say but I can't, so I just roll my eyes.

'It won't matter much in the grand scheme of things,' Owl Man sighs, 'but it's better to spare a life than take it. And perhaps my father will calm down when Claudia carries news of this back to him. Knowing he's defeated, maybe he'll retreat to his base as requested, where he can do no further damage.'

'Or maybe he'll tear through the streets of London

and kill everyone he can find before the chance is denied him,' Dr Oystein notes.

'Maybe,' Owl Man says glumly. 'There's never any telling for certain with him.'

The men – uncle and nephew, the lord of destruction and his heir – stare at the corpses on the street for a while, as if thinking of all the bodies they've been responsible for over the years. Then Sakarias whines and nudges Owl Man's legs, looking for permission to chow down.

'No,' he says, snapping back into the present. 'We don't have time for that. We must press on. There might be other mutants in the area. If Claudia finds them and they use their walkie-talkies to summon Mr Dowling . . .'

'You should have thought about that before you let her waltz out of here,' Rage says, but Owl Man ignores the jibe and looks questioningly at Dr Oystein.

The doc is silent for a few more seconds, lost in his memories. Then he sniffs and starts for the front door. 'Come,' he says.

'Where?' Owl Man asks.

'My laboratory. It will be a fitting venue for the final revelations.'

'If I might make a suggestion?' Owl Man murmurs. 'The streets are not secure. There's a boat out back. It would make more sense to use that.'

'But it's only a short distance,' Dr Oystein says.

'The final stretch can sometimes be the most treacherous,' Owl Man replies. 'We don't want to run any unnecessary risks this close to ultimate victory.'

'A bit late to be thinking about that now,' Rage snorts but again Owl Man ignores him.

Dr Oystein nods thoughtfully. 'You are right as usual, Zachary. Besides, it is a fine night for a trip down the river. Lead the way, please, Rage.'

'My pleasure, cap'n,' Rage grins. 'But I still think it was madness letting the girl go.'

'Is there no room for compassion in your heart?' Dr Oystein asks tetchily.

'Not since I found out that the so-called saviour of the world was a traitor and a hypocrite,' Rage says cheerfully, and the doc looks like he wants to cry when he hears that.

'Come, Becky,' Owl Man says, extending a hand to help me to my feet. 'You may move about again, but I forbid you to attack Dr Oystein, myself or any of our associates.'

I ignore his hand and push myself to my feet. I try to throw a punch at him, but every muscle in my arm tenses at the thought. I try to lean over and bite into his throat, but my legs take root and my jaw clamps shut. Scowling, I accept the limits that he's placed on me and point to my lips instead.

'What?' he asks. Then he remembers and laughs. 'Oh, I see. Yes, you can talk again too.'

'You no-good, worthless son of a –' I start to yell.

'But softly,' Owl Man stops me. 'And no swearing or vile threats.'

I snarl at him, then push past in disgust, heading out back where Rage is waiting. Just before I exit, I pause and glance at Barnes, lying dead on the floor in a congealing pool of blood. I feel angry, guilty and helpless. There's so much I want to say to him, but all I can manage is a weak, worthless, 'Sorry.'

Rage helps me down into the small boat moored outside, acting like the gentleman he isn't. I wince as I climb in. My energy has dwindled and the pain is kicking in hard again. Dr Oystein notices my discomfort.

'Do you still have the syringes that you took from me?' he asks.

I'd almost forgotten about those. He brought three syringes to the brewery, each filled with a concentrated version of the energising gloop from the Groove Tubes. He injected me with the contents of one. I took the other two in case I needed them later.

'I left them on the counter,' I tell him.

'Rage, would you be so good as to fetch them for us?' Dr Oystein asks.

'Anything to oblige,' Rage says, and shoots back into the bar. He returns with the syringes a moment later and passes them to the doc. He prepares one and gestures for me to extend my arm.

'I can do it myself,' I grunt, reaching for the syringe.

Dr Oystein shakes his head. 'A syringe can be a weapon. Alas, I know that better than most. Let me do this for you, B. It's not that I don't trust my nephew's hypnotic spell, but you're a resourceful girl and I worry that you might find a way to countermand his orders.'

I pull a face, wishing I could take the syringe and plunge the tip of the needle into the doc's eyeball, then slip overboard in the confusion. But Owl Man's hold over me is total and, regardless of the doc's high opinion of me, I'm not *that* resourceful.

I'm still in the tattered remains of my wedding dress, which doesn't have any sleeves, so I simply stick out my arm and look away glumly. As Dr Oystein injects me, Rage casts off and we drift out into the centre of the river. There's an engine on the boat, but he doesn't start it. I suppose they don't want to draw unwelcome attention.

'Where to, doc?' Rage asks breezily.

'East,' Dr Oystein grunts, telling Rage no more than he needs to, clearly suspicious of him. Rage might be all sweetness and light now, but we know from past experience that he can change sides whenever it suits him.

Rage picks up the oars which were lying on the floor of the boat, moves to the front and starts rowing, slowly, making as little noise as possible. Sakarias looks over the side, studying its reflection. It barks softly, leans further over and laps at the water, then settles back beside its master. The dog is close to me too, so I run my hands through its fur, finding comfort in that.

Dr Oystein's gaze is distant for a while, as it was in the pub. Then he smiles wearily and returns to the story that he was telling before we were interrupted. 'Albrecht was unaware of my true intentions for a long time. We worked as a team for many years. I trusted him completely and he trusted me.

'Our most crucial work was conducted in private. We were wary of allowing others access to our secrets. Zachary was the first outsider we let into our world. We trusted him because he was family, the one surviving child of Albrecht's.'

'But you told us you had nothing to do with your nephew after the war,' I note, remembering the doc's original story.

Dr Oystein sighs. 'We had not planned to involve him. He'd been adopted by an English family, which is how he came to be named Tom White. We thought he would be safer if we steered clear of him. For years we let him lead his own life.

'Then Zachary began conducting his own genetic experiments. The acorn, as the saying goes, had not fallen far from the tree. While his work had nothing to do with zombies, we could see that he would be of great value to us. We were sure he could help us unlock puzzles which had previously hindered our research.'

'You're too kind,' Owl Man mutters. 'You would have advanced without me.'

'Probably.' Dr Oystein smiles. 'Zachary was intrigued when we introduced him to our work, hiring him without revealing ourselves. Later, when we met and told him who we were, that interest became a passion and he dedicated himself to our cause. We felt like a family again. It was a joyful, exciting time.

'Then Albrecht learnt that I had developed the zombie-killing virus.'

Dr Oystein's features cloud over and he starts rubbing Sakarias too. The dog pants happily, delighted with all the attention.

'He was furious,' the doc whispers. 'He could not understand why I had kept such a thing from him.'

Oystein tried to explain it to his angry brother. He told Albrecht that he felt their mission was to cleanse this planet of the living and install the babies in their place. Albrecht thought that Oystein was crazy. (And he wasn't wrong there!) He told his brother to give him the virus, so that he could release it. Oystein refused to hand over his precious vial. He wouldn't even tell Albrecht where it was stored. The brothers argued fiercely and eventually came to blows.

Oystein wasn't a natural fighter, whereas Albrecht had boxed to a high amateur standard in his youth. While it was by no means one-sided, Albrecht had the beating of his desperate brother, so Oystein resorted to dirty tactics.

'We were in Albrecht's part of the laboratory,' the doc says. 'He threw me against a cabinet. The glass shattered. There were bottles and syringes inside. I tossed a few bottles at him, but he swatted them aside. As he moved in to attack again, I grabbed the nearest needle and jabbed it into his throat. I meant only to wound him, to buy time and space for myself. But I instinctively pressed down on the plunger and injected him with whatever was in the syringe.'

The doc falls silent again, but this time shows no signs of recovering his voice. His fingers withdraw from the dog's fur and settle on his knees, where they curl into talons of remorse.

Owl Man takes up the story. 'My father had developed various strains of the mutant gene. Oystein and I had been involved in some of the experiments, but most were a mystery to us. The liquid in the syringe didn't kill Albrecht, but left him in an inbetween state, not undead but not truly alive either. It also dissolved many of the cells inside my father's brain, driving him to madness.'

Rage hoots with delight. 'You mean Mr Dowling's a nutter because of what the doc did to him?'

'Yes,' Owl Man says sadly. 'He was driven insane at the hand of his brother, and the pair have been at war ever since.'

I stare at Owl Man, then at the doc, who is shivering and gazing out over the water blankly. I try to imagine what that must have been like, to have destroyed the mind of the person you cared about most in the world. And despite all that I know about him, and everything he has done, in that moment I feel sorrier for Dr Oystein than I do for any other wretched soul on this wreck of a planet.

FIVE

We follow a bend in the river, the towers of Canary Wharf standing tall and proud above us, looking like they've been moved here from New York or Tokyo. There was an underground shopping centre beneath the skyscrapers. I bet it's now packed with zombie bankers and stockbrokers, nearly as ghoulish and harmful in death as they were in life.

Owl Man catches my smile and cocks his head. 'Something amuses you?'

'Lots of things amuse me,' I tell him, letting the smile spread. 'The thought of your head on a pole, or seeing an asteroid land on Rage and squash him like an ant.'

'It's good that you have not lost your sense of humour,' he says.

'That'll be the last thing I lose,' I boast. 'When you've stripped everything else away, I'll still be chuckling. I'll take this grin to the grave.'

'I hope so,' he says earnestly. 'I've grown surprisingly fond of you, Becky Smith. I would like to think that when you pass you do so on your own terms, with no regrets. Really, in the end, that is the most any of us can hope for.'

'You're wrong,' I tell him.

'Oh?'

'We can hope to take some others down with us,' I smirk.

Owl Man giggles, sounding for a moment like Dan-Dan. I stare at the weird-looking man more closely.

'Where were you when all this was going on?' I ask.

'When my father was fighting with my uncle?' He sighs. 'I was at work in another part of the lab.'

'I mean afterwards, when Mr Dowling ran away. I'm guessing he ran?'

'Oh yes,' Owl Man says glumly. 'As his mind caved in on itself, he ran as if he was on fire. In a way, he has never stopped running.'

Owl Man crosses his legs. Sakarias looks up to make sure its master is comfortable, then relaxes again.

'Forgive the cliché, but I found myself on the horns of a dilemma,' he says. 'I loved and admired both men. I was distraught when my father severed all ties with us and set off down his own mad path. Oystein did not share all of the details with me. I think it would be fair to say that you massaged the facts to suit your story?'

He throws the question to Dr Oystein, but the doc ignores it, submerged in his own lonely little world. Owl Man grunts and continues.

'I guessed there was more to it than I had been told. I carried on working for my uncle, but tracked down my father on the sly. He was in a mess, even more out of control than he is today, but determined to strike back. He had lost interest in the living. In his crazed state, he craved chaos.'

Albrecht had bounced back swiftly from his total

mental collapse. He hadn't found his new persona yet – the clown costume was many years away – but he'd regained his basic faculties and set his sights on pitching the world into a crazy mess, to mirror the rocky realm of his troubled mind.

The deranged Dowling brother decided to let Oystein unleash the hounds of Hell, but he was determined to keep the living around too. He longed for war, an eternal struggle between the living and the undead, so that he could cavort at the centre with his army of mutants.

'Obviously I knew that Albrecht was insane,' Owl Man says, 'but he was the only person who had the power to stop Oystein from wiping out the human race.'

'You cared about the living?' I ask sceptically.

Owl Man chews at his inner cheek. 'Honestly? No. I never truly did, even when I was one of them. I always felt detached from ordinary people. But I relished the *extraordinary*. The minds of rare individuals like Albrecht and Oystein were magnificent jewels. I was worried that we might lose them forever, that my uncle would produce a race of drab, unimaginative, soulless clones.'

Owl Man decided to tread a dangerous line, to serve two masters at once, and work for both of the brothers as they continued with their experiments. He helped where he could, as he had before, but also served as spy and censor.

'If I felt that one of them was heading down a damaging route, I tinkered with results and spoiled their experiments,' he explains. 'For instance, when Oystein was close to perfecting a virus that would wipe out humanity, I subtly interfered and distracted him.'

But Owl Man knew that the doc would make the breakthrough in the end and produce the virus that would rid the world of its *human stain*. He wouldn't dare release it until Albrecht had made progress with his babies – Oystein was afraid to remove all evidence of *Homo sapiens* from the history books before his brother had lined up their replacements – but time was running out.

'Hold on,' I stop Owl Man. 'If that's true, then if Mr Dowling had stopped trying to clone babies, Dr

Oystein would never have released the virus. Why didn't you convince him to stop?'

'I suggested that,' Owl Man says, 'but the babies fascinated him, and by that stage he lived only to satisfy his own interests. He didn't want to stop Oystein totally, merely halt him at a certain point and hold him there.'

As Mr Dowling got close to cloning a crop of mutant babies, Owl Man knew it was time to make a decision. He could no longer walk a tightrope between his father and his uncle. He had to choose.

'As much as it pained me, I betrayed Oystein,' Owl Man says. 'My plan was to kill him and take his place. I hoped to then keep Albrecht in check by convincing him of the merits of a different strategy. He was hell-bent on chaos, but I felt that he could achieve that without creating an army of the undead. If he built up his mutant forces, and added scores of cloned babies to the mix, they could start a war with humanity and keep it running as long as he wished.'

'Hardly paradise on Earth,' I growl.

'Not an ideal situation,' Owl Man agrees, 'but it

would have been better than what we have now, billions killed, the living dead running wild across the globe. Sometimes the lesser of two evils is the most that we can aim for.

'My attempt on Oystein's life failed,' he continues, 'but I managed to make off with a sample of Schlesinger-10, which I found hidden away. I handed the vial over to my father, acting as if that had been my goal all along — he didn't know that I had meant to thwart him. The gift pleased him at the time, then utterly delighted him later, when we came to realise how unique the sample was.'

'What do you mean?' I frown. 'Schlesinger-10 isn't unique. The doc must have loads of the stuff knocking around.' I stare at Owl Man, feeling a sudden sinking feeling in the pit where my stomach used to be. 'Doesn't he?'

Owl Man shakes his head. 'It was a one-off success, a chance quirk that he was unable to repeat, no matter how many times he tried.'

'Bullshit,' Rage snorts. 'You're telling me he came up with the formula and then forgot it?'

'Certain chemicals reacted in a way that they never have again,' Owl Man says. 'There must have been something mixed in with one of the solutions. He was never able to figure out what that was.'

'That's why he was so desperate to retrieve it,' I groan. 'He didn't have any of the human-killing virus himself.'

Owl Man looks confused for a moment. Then he smiles. 'Oh, that's right, you think –'

'Enough,' Dr Oystein snaps, and Owl Man winces and falls silent. I guess the doc has had his fill of listening about his one great failure.

'Let me get this straight,' Rage mutters. 'There's only one vial of the human-killing virus in the world, and Becky has delivered it to the one person whose goal is to release it.' He catches my eye and laughs. 'Good going, girl. You couldn't have made more of a balls-up of this if you'd tried. This is the end of humanity, and it's all Becky Smith's fault.

'You know what?' a beaming Rage adds as I glower at him. 'It's days like this that make it worth getting out of bed!'

SIX

I'm sickened by what I've done, the way I've played into Dr Oystein's hands. I spend the rest of the boat ride trying to break Owl Man's hold over me. I want to hurl myself at the doc, knock him overboard, drag him to the bottom of the river and crack his head open as we go. But my body rejects my command every time. I'm fighting a lost battle, but I don't let that stop me, trying and trying and trying again to free myself of Owl Man's mental shackles.

As we draw close to the pier for the O2, Dr

Oystein stirs and tells Rage to dock. I glance up at the famous landmark. It's always reminded me of a giant Frisbee with a load of spikes sticking out of it. My dad used to call it an eyesore, and for once I agree with him.

We get out of the boat, Owl Man pausing to whisper in my ear, 'Stay close and be a good girl.' It's not a request, and I find myself sticking by his side, an obedient little puppy.

We advance on the dome and I wonder if the doc is taking us in to catch a concert. Maybe he's put together an undead band and wants to rock out as he brings the world to its end.

But he doesn't aim for the regular entrance. Instead he circles round until he comes to what looks like a service door, covered in electricity symbols and warnings to keep out. He produces a key, unlocks the door, and we step into a small room filled with machinery and a high-pitched whining sound that sends nasty shivers down my spine.

Dr Oystein hurries to a wall of pipes and controls,

and presses a few buttons. There's a clicking noise and a crack appears down one side of the wall. As the doc pushes forward, I realise the wall is set on hinges, like a swinging door. We follow him into a brightly lit corridor and the wall swings shut behind us. It's instantly much quieter.

At the end of the corridor we come to a set of stairs and head down until we reach a platform overlooking a series of cubic rooms, each encased with glass walls and ceilings. There must be dozens of these cells, each neatly ordered, filled with scientific equipment, test tubes of all shapes and sizes, storage files and more. People are beavering away in some of them, living scientists by their look and smell. They ignore us and concentrate on their work.

'My laboratory,' Dr Oystein says, smiling fondly. 'I had this place built when they were constructing the Millennium Dome, as it was originally called. It seemed like the perfect place to base myself.'

'I've gotta hand it to you, doc,' Rage says, 'this is

well cool. It looks like a villain's secret hideout in a James Bond film.'

Dr Oystein chuckles. 'I must admit, I was a fan of those movies, and they influenced the style that I requested of my architects.'

'How did you keep this secret?' I frown. 'This is a major public building. There must have been TV cameras filming it all the time as it went up.'

'Secrets are best hidden in plain view,' the doc says. 'With all the work going on, it was easy to slip in a few extra teams unnoticed. You can get away with anything if you have the right contacts. And I had the very best.'

The doc starts to descend and we trail along behind. On the ground floor he walks past some of the cells, explaining their purpose, what the equipment is for, the experiments he has conducted in them, what his teams are working on now.

'This is a particularly important room,' he says at one point, stopping before a cell that looks no different to the others, except for large, sophisticated freezers set along three of the walls. 'The freezing units are full of embryos waiting to be fertilised. There are more in similar laboratories worldwide.'

'You mean you're making mutant babies like Mr Dowling's?' I ask.

'No,' he says. 'These will be ordinary human babies.'

I stare at him uncertainly. 'I don't get it. I thought you wanted to replace the living. Are you telling us you plan to resurrect humanity?'

Dr Oystein shakes his head. 'Humans were given enough chances. We must never allow them to hold sway again.'

The doc turns slowly, casting his gaze around the clinical glass complex.

'Albrecht's babies are the future,' he says. 'But they will need to be guided and directed in their early years. It will be a long time before they're ready to take their place as the new rulers of this planet.

'I realised early on that we should not delay the elimination of the living while we waited for the babies to mature, as Albrecht's cloned children might be tainted by humans' bad habits. But we couldn't simply abandon the infants either, so young and defenceless.'

'The babies?' I snort. 'Defenceless? Hardly! They're deadlier than a shoal of piranhas.'

'In certain ways,' Dr Oystein admits. 'But in other ways they're helpless, and will be for decades to come. They will need guardians, people who love them, who will raise them to be pure and true. I couldn't trust adults to serve that purpose. But I could trust –'

'– children,' I finish with an understanding growl.

Dr Oystein nods. 'My Angels. So named because I wanted them to be *guardian* angels. Children and teenagers who had not been warped by the world of their elders, who believed in justice, truth, honesty, goodness.'

'Like you?' I sneer. 'A guy who lies to the people who love and serve him, who cheats and kills them if he has to?'

Dr Oystein's gaze drops. 'Your accusations hurt

me,' he says softly, 'but only because they are valid. I *am* a liar, a cheat, a killer. The things I have done are beyond forgiveness, even though I have done them in God's name, for the sake of this world's future.

'I will not live to see the fruit of my handiwork,' he goes on. 'I will step aside soon. I am of the old breed, and there should be no place for my kind in the new world. The Angels will take my place. Knowing nothing of my deception and dark deeds, they'll carry the spark of hope that I instilled in them, and fan it fully into life.

'I promised to release you from your pain when our work here is finished,' the doc says quietly. 'Perhaps I will set my own soul free at the same time. I doubt it will go to the same place as yours – I fear I shall never see the gates of Heaven – but it will be a relief to put this ghastly business behind me.'

I stare at the doc, disturbed and confused. 'You don't want to set yourself up as president or emperor or whatever?'

'Perish the thought,' he snorts. 'My aim has been to tear down the rotting foundations of the old world and clear the way for a fresh start. I see no part for myself in the gleaming new society that is to come.'

'That's why I returned to the fold,' Owl Man says. 'It became evident, after I failed to kill my uncle, that he was going to release the virus that would turn billions of people into zombies. He had the backing of powerful figures across the globe. The process had been set in motion and could not be stopped. So I worked with him again, covertly, to do what I could to ensure that the apocalypse passed with as few glitches as possible.'

'We needed to bring things to a head,' Dr Oystein says. 'Albrecht had been avoiding direct conflict. I had to set the undead against the living to bring him out of hiding. Chaos would lure him into opposition and force a showdown. I had faith that the vial of Schlesinger-10 would resurface, as it has. Now we are free to press ahead. We will rid the world of its human curse, track down my brother and put him out of his misery, take the babies into our care and re-educate them, build a race of leaders worthy of this magnificent globe.'

'That's all well and good,' Rage sniffs, 'but it doesn't explain why you have all these human eggs on ice.'

'Ah yes, the embryos.' The doc smiles. 'I knew there must be a bridge between the reign of humanity and the babies. My Angels will be that bridge. It will be a hundred years or more before the babies come of age and are fit to rule. They'll be able to sustain themselves during that time. They don't need to eat often, and they can eat anything. Revitaliseds, on the other hand, need brains and, while we have enough stored away to last for many years, the supply won't last indefinitely.'

My eyes widen. 'You're going to breed humans,' I gasp. 'To serve as fodder for your Angels.'

'Yes,' Dr Oystein says. 'We'll grow them in facilities like this one, ten or twenty years from now, when the human-killing virus is no longer active. A crop of babies every nine months. We will let them grow for a year or two, then harvest them. Brains for all. The fuel that my Angels will need to oversee the building of the new world.'

'Yum-yum,' Owl Man murmurs, licking his lips, and, at that, even the usually unshockable Rage looks queasy.

SEVEN

'You're a monster,' I tell the doc.

'Yes,' he says glumly. 'I have had to become one.'

'No,' I retort. 'Don't try that crap on me. It's not something you've been forced to do. You've chosen this path. You've already killed billions of people. Now you're going to target the rest of them, then breed specimens just to eat. It's because you enjoy it, because you're sick in the head, even more so than your messed-up brother.'

'You misjudge me,' Dr Oystein says. 'This gives me no pleasure. I am simply doing what is required.'

The doc taps the glass and points to the embryos in the freezers. 'Each egg, once fertilised, has the potential to be a messenger of peace and love, a prophet, a saint, a philanthropist. But we all know that most would turn out to be vicious, self-centred and petty. History tells us this. Ever since the beginning of time, we have been creatures of conflict and hate.

'World War II was the final nail in the coffin. It was clear that the situation had spun out of control. I did not even need the atomic bombings of Hiroshima and Nagasaki to prove the point for me. We were on a one-way road to destruction and we were going to take the entire planet down with us.

'Life is a gift, B, and we have abused it from the start. There have been sparks of hope along the way, good people who showed us that we are not all bitter and cruel. But too little goodness, spread too thinly.

'I want to bring to this world the peace that the great prophets tried and failed to introduce. God hoped to show us the way through honest, decent people. When that failed, He decided to operate through a base, monstrous creature instead. *Me*.'

Dr Oystein turns away from the freezers and starts walking again. We follow in silence, listening numbly as he makes his pitiful case.

'It's a shame that the human race didn't choose the path of truth and light, but I'm a realist and, if billions must be sacrificed to heal this world's wounds, so be it. The babies will become the upstanding citizens that the rest of us have failed to be. My Angels will teach them to be good, and there will be no wars over land, race or religion, because those things will have no meaning any more.

'Don't you see?' he cries. 'The babies won't overpopulate the planet or poison rivers, oceans, the air. They won't hunt animals to extinction or tear down forests to make a profit. They won't go to war or persecute their fellow beings.

'They'll continue to make scientific advances, and aim for the stars, as humanity has since we first began to dream. But they'll do so because they want to spread love and joy, not because they yearn to conquer.'

'Hippy twaddle,' Rage mutters, then grimaces. I don't think he meant to speak his thoughts out loud.

'Perhaps,' Dr Oystein says with a little dip of his head. 'But this world has been in pain for a long time. I believe that I've found a cure for its ills. If you consider it logically, without letting your emotions get in the way, you might find yourself starting to side with me, despite your moral objections.'

'Never,' I snap.

'You won't even give me a chance?' Dr Oystein asks sadly.

'Nope.'

He shrugs. 'That is probably as it should be. You are tied to your path as I am tied to mine. I won't claim that I knew how important you were when I first met you, but it swiftly became clear, even before I learnt of your link to Albrecht and the babies.'

I frown. 'You didn't know?'

'No,' he says. 'Zachary never told me.'

I glance at Owl Man with surprise and he pulls a *whoops!* expression. Then he laughs. 'I returned to the fold, Becky, but I continued to work for my father as well as for my uncle. I had erred before, so I acknowledged that if I'd been wrong once, I might be wrong again. I tried to keep an open mind, to work with Oystein but to question our actions at every stage. I thought it would be dangerous to tell him of Albrecht's love for you, or that the babies saw you as their mother.

'But, as destiny brought you, my father and the babies ever closer together, I saw that I was a fool to stand in its way. You have been the key from the start, the only one who could penetrate Albrecht's defences, find the missing vial and return it to us. I'm not sure if it's the hand of God or a quirk of fate, but your purpose from the day you drew your first breath has been to lead us to this moment.'

'You're a goddess,' Dr Oystein says softly. 'You will bring death to this world, as many gods and goddesses of legend did, but you'll also bring fresh life and hope to its shores. You are the mother of the future and the executioner of the past, our greatest dread and our most glorious triumph.'

'How's that for flattery?' Rage laughs as I gawp at the pair of beaming men. 'Don't worry, Becky, to me you're still an ugly, charmless troll. I won't be building a shrine to you any time soon.'

'Thank heaven for that,' I sneer, then shake my head at the doc and his nephew. 'You two are lunatics.'

Dr Oystein smiles again, then stops at the door of a room with lots of laden bookshelves. 'If so, this is where our lunacy reaches its towering crescendo.'

The doc pushes the door open and goes to a shelf. There are several Bibles on it. He takes one down and lays it on a table. Stares at it with a look that's half love, half fear.

'Gods and goddesses cannot work alone,' he mutters. 'They need help from their human servants. We all have a part to play. Zachary and I knew that destiny might require a helping hand. So when he was hypnotising you, he ...'

The doc raises an eyebrow and Owl Man takes over.

'I have spent decades studying my father's mind. Because of our natural bond, he let me get close to him, but he never granted me access to the most intimate levels of his mental universe. Even so, I had a good idea of how to penetrate his defences, assuming one could get close enough to strike the first blow.'

'You set me up to attack him!' I shout, seeing it now. 'You stuck some sort of a time bomb inside my head, so that when we married and he opened himself up to me, I'd rip the location of the vial from him.'

'Yes,' Owl Man says proudly. 'It wasn't easy. You will have no recollection of it, but I had you under my wing for the better part of two weeks. I had to prime you, then hide all traces of my interference. We couldn't be sure that it would work, but we did the best job we could.'

'After that we had to trust in fate,' Dr Oystein says. 'We were tempted to push you towards

Albrecht, but he would have seen through such designs. Being so paranoid, he can sniff out a trap from miles away. So we did nothing to pitch you together. We were sure you would find your way to him in time. As I said earlier, you are a creature of destiny. This was always going to happen. It was simply a matter of when and how.'

'They make a persuasive case,' Rage murmurs.

'They're nutters,' I snarl.

'Yeah, but the way it went down . . . me finding out the truth about the doc . . . teaming up with Dan-Dan . . . you following us to Battersea . . . If I wasn't an atheist, I'd say that was all too much to be mere coincidence.'

I grin bleakly. 'You know what they say — it's a funny old world.'

'Anyway,' Dr Oystein concludes, 'that brings us to where we are now. All that remains is for us to see this through to its preordained finale. It's time for you to hand over the vial that you took from my brother. Then we can draw a line in the sand, bid the living farewell, and take our first tentative steps forward.'

The doc opens up the Bible. I see that it's hollow inside. Something nestles within. He tenderly prises the object out of its resting place and I spot a vial full of a dark red liquid. He shakes it at me. Pretends to drop it. Laughs when I gasp.

'It would not matter if it fell,' he says. 'The container would hold. You'd need a jackhammer to even dent it.'

'Is that Clements-13?' I croak, even though I know it's a stupid question.

'Yes,' he says, his smile fading. 'The two viruses, together at last.'

I stare at the vial, fixated. I don't know why he's shown it to us, why he's taken this risk and flashed his ace card when there was no need. He's hidden the zombie-destroying virus all this time. Why display it now?

But this is my big chance. If I can swipe it from him, remove the outer tubes, smash open the inner vial and release the zombie-eliminating fumes . . .

'Easy,' Owl Man murmurs as I strain against his hold over me.

Dr Oystein holds out the vial of Clements-13, gently teasing me. 'Come now, B,' he says sweetly. 'The time for games is over. This is where we get serious. I have shown you mine. Now you need to show me yours.

'Pass me the vial of Schlesinger-10, please.'

EIGHT

All three stare at me expectantly, waiting for me to hand over the poison which will bring the human era to a swift and fatal end. I stare back solemnly at the doc, saying nothing, milking the moment.

Then I grin wickedly and shoot him the finger.

Dr Oystein's face darkens. 'Do not toy with me,' he growls.

'Get stuffed,' I jeer.

'Becky!' Owl Man barks. 'Give him the vial.'

'You can get stuffed too,' I retort with undeniable relish.

Owl Man blinks with shock.

Dr Oystein snaps, 'Has she broken your hold over her?'

'She must have,' Owl Man mutters, 'but I do not know how.'

'Don't sweat it, Owlie,' I smirk. 'If I had free will, I'd be ripping your brains out. You're still the boss of me, worse luck.'

'Then give him the vial,' Owl Man says slowly, sternly, his voice resonating deeply.

'Can't,' I beam. Then I hit them with the kicker. 'I don't have it.'

Rage howls with laughter as the men gawp. 'Trust Queen B to come up with a kick-in-the-nuts twist!'

'But you told us you had it,' Dr Oystein wheezes, ignoring the gleeful Rage.

'No,' I correct him. 'You asked me if I'd taken it from Mr Dowling. I said I had, which was the truth. I also told you I'd hidden it in the cavity of my stomach, which was true too. But you never asked me if I *still* had it.'

Dr Oystein looks as if he's about to throw up. Owl Man has started to tremble. Rage carries on laughing.

'You set it aside?' the doc croaks.

'Yeah,' I drawl.

'Where is it?' he asks.

'Don't know,' I answer innocently.

'Zachary!' he yells, losing his temper.

'Tell us where it is,' Owl Man says gravely.

'I can't,' I reply sweetly. 'Like I said, I don't know.'

'But you must!' Dr Oystein howls. Sakarias is startled by the noise and growls angrily at the doctor.

'But I don't,' I smile.

Dr Oystein raises a hand to strike me. Owl Man coughs politely and says, 'No, uncle. That is not your way. You will regret it if you hit her.' As the doc practically foams at the mouth, Owl Man faces me. 'Tell us what you did with the vial, Becky.'

'Well, since you asked nicely . . .' I simper, then shrug. 'When I saw that County Hall had fallen, I lost hope. I thought the *good doctor* was done for, that Mr Dowling had killed him. I was sure my vengeful husband would track me down and retrieve his precious vial. I wanted to thwart him.

'So I gave the vial to Holy Moly. I told the loveable little beast that if it wanted to please its mummy, it should take the vial deep underground and hide it in a place where nobody would ever find it.

'You're back where you started, doc. The vial's lost to you, out of sight, out of reach. How does *that* tickle your fancy, creep?'

NINE

Dr Oystein's face crumples and his body sags. It's like he's folding in on himself. There's a chair behind the table and he sinks into it, clutching the vial of Clements-13 to his chest, staring off into space.

I pick up the hollowed Bible and smile at the cover. 'So much for the Good Book,' I smirk, then slam it down on the table.

'What a girl,' Rage whoops. He's loving this. Rage is like Mr Dowling, a relisher of chaos. It doesn't matter that he's allied himself with Owl Man and Dr Oystein. He can still admire a tasty piece of trickery.

'A most unfortunate and unexpected twist,' Owl Man murmurs. 'But one that is not as cruel a blow as you suspect. This is not the end for us, uncle. In fact, it now frees us to push ahead as we would have years ago if not for the bind which Albrecht had us in.'

Dr Oystein stares at Owl Man blankly, as if he doesn't understand the language.

'Do you want to pass the vial of Clements-13 to me?' Owl Man asks quietly. 'I can take care of it for you.'

That seems like a strange request, but maybe he's worried that the doc will lose his mind and accidentally open the vial and spill the zombie-destroying liquid in his distressed state.

Dr Oystein looks at the vial, thinks for a moment, then shakes his head. 'No.'

Owl Man frowns. 'Are you sure? I think this is the time to –'

'No!' Dr Oystein shouts. He points a finger at Owl Man and starts to tear into him. But then he collects himself and smiles shakily. 'No, Zachary. You are right. This is not the end. But we must be careful. As you said earlier, the last few steps can be the most treacherous. We should think this through before acting.'

The doc places the vial of Clements-13 on the table and stares at the red liquid, immersed in his thoughts. For a long time silence reigns. Finally he looks at us again and his expression clears.

'We could have targeted Albrecht years ago, but I was worried that if we killed him, we would never find where he had hidden his sample of Schlesinger-10. Without it, we face a long, hard, hand-to-hand war with the human survivors, and I doubt we will ever fully wipe them from the face of the planet.

'Now that Albrecht has lost his key prize, there's nothing to stop us hunting my brother, storming his den, finishing him off and taking control of the babies. It would be a harsh battle, with many casualties on both sides, but I'm sure we would be triumphant. That's what Zachary meant when he said that we're free to push ahead.

'But the vial of Schlesinger-10 is even more important to us than the babies. We need it to ensure victory over the living. Without it, we cannot shield the babies from their interference, and I fear that history will repeat itself, and the babies will grow up to mimic the destructive ways of their human forebears.

'I think we still have a chance to recover the vial. The babies see Albrecht as their father. I'm not convinced that the one you call Holy Moly will obey your wishes. It will probably return the sample of Schlesinger-10 to Albrecht. If it does, and we hit his base swiftly, we might be able to catch him before he can hide it again.'

Owl Man is staring at Dr Oystein oddly, head cocked. He looks like he wants to ask a question, but the doc waves a hand at him and he says nothing.

'If Holy Moly *has* hidden the vial as you requested, an attack might compel it to change its mind. If we threaten Albrecht, the baby might return the vial to its father. If my brother got his hands on it again, and escaped, our stalemate would be resumed. Maybe we should do nothing, keep our eyes open, let the dust settle, and try to set a trap for the baby further down the line. If we could capture it and convince it to reveal the location of the vial . . .'

Dr Oystein thinks about this in silence for a long time. Finally he stands.

'We will gamble and take the offensive. If we find Albrecht with the Schlesinger-10 in his possession, we'll kill him and take it. If the baby has hidden it, we'll eliminate Albrecht and deal with the infant afterwards — perhaps B can persuade it to give us the vial. In the worst-case scenario, if Albrecht has regained his prize and stashed it in a secret hiding place, or stands poised, ready to open it, we'll retreat and hope that another opportunity to retrieve the liquid presents itself.'

Dr Oystein starts to put the Clements-13 back into the Bible. Then he stops and studies it uncertainly. He looks at Rage and me. 'But what to do with this? I could leave it here, where it has sat safely all this time, but Rage and B know about it now. If our paths diverge, one of them might return and steal it, and use it to destroy all of the living dead.'

The doc chuckles ruefully. 'I should not have shown my hand before making sure that you had the vial of Schlesinger-10. I thought this was the final act. I behaved like one of those silly Bond villains, revealing too much when the battle had yet to be decided.'

The doc thinks about it some more, then sticks the vial of zombie-eradicating liquid in one of his pockets. 'I'll keep it with me,' he says. 'It will be as safe on my person as it will be anywhere. It might even prove useful. If we fall foul of Albrecht's army, and he pins us down, I can use it to force him to let us go.'

Dr Oystein flashes a smile at me. 'Perhaps I did not act so rashly. In retrospect, I think I was prompted to reveal my hidden sample of Clements-13. God knew what you had done with your vial, Becky, and He gently nudged me to bring mine out into the light, knowing that I might have need of it soon.'

'Sure,' I say sarcastically. 'It was all God's doing. Only a lunatic would think any differently.'

The doc doesn't rise to the bait. Instead he starts for the door, telling Owl Man to follow, ticking off on his fingers the things that they need to do. He's all business now, fully focused on the battle to come, confident of victory, a twisted angel on a demonic mission.

TEN

We use Barnes's boat to cross the river, then make our way through the streets to Bow. The doc and Owl Man are nervous, afraid the babies or mutants will spot us if they're still abroad. But the city is quiet. The zombies have retreated ahead of the spreading sunlight and there's no sign of Mr Dowling or his troops. They're either searching for me elsewhere or they've retired, as Owl Man suggested, to consider their next course of action.

I want to bolt for freedom, but Owl Man hasn't given me permission to stray, so I'm still bound close to his side. He's also ordered my silence again, so that I can't betray them if we have to hide. I keep trying to break free, to lash out at him and slit his throat, but he's sunk his hooks deep inside my brain, where I can't rip them loose.

After a short trek, we arrive at the gates of the Bow Quarter. Once a factory and then expensive flats, my dad called it the Beverly Hills of the East End. Now it's been turned into a makeshift base for Dr Oystein's Angels.

The revitaliseds come out to gawp as we enter. I don't know what the doc told them about me, whether they think I'm mad or a traitor. All they know for sure is that I attacked their leader, Rage slaughtered two of their friends, and Owl Man is a long-standing enemy. They're not happy to see any of us and I understand why.

The doc pauses in the middle of an open area and beckons the Angels forward. I spot some familiar faces among the mix, my room-mates Ashtat, Shane and Carl, the twins Cian and Awnya, Ingrid and Ivor. Master Zhang is present too, along with the living

Ciara and Reilly – a dinner lady and an ex-soldier – who are standing slightly apart from the others, holding hands and looking worried.

'Say nothing,' Owl Man murmurs as the glaring Angels gather around us.

'Good news, my children,' Dr Oystein says brightly. 'B has returned. Rage has too, as you can see, along with another unexpected guest.'

There's an uneasy silence. The Angels are looking at me dubiously, at Owl Man fearfully, at Rage with outright hostility.

'He killed Pearse and Conall,' Ivor mutters.

'Yes,' Dr Oystein says evenly.

'Are you saying that doesn't matter, that he's one of us again?' Ivor presses. Ivor has a great talent for picking locks, but right now his fingers are twitching in a very different way, and I bet he'd love to drive them through Rage's eyes.

Dr Oystein chuckles wryly. 'Sadly, no. I had high hopes for Rage, but I was wrong to trust him. He is no longer an Angel.'

Rage stiffens. He gets the sense that he might be a

sacrificial lamb and he glances about, looking for a place to run. My spirits perk up at the thought of seeing Rage getting his comeuppance. But then the doc spoils it all.

'That being said, he can still serve a noble purpose. While I can never forgive him for what he did to Pearse and Conall, we need his assistance in the battle to come. He will help us, not because he cares for our cause, but because it suits him. He is here to serve his own selfish needs and that is why we can trust him for the moment.'

The doc turns in a circle to address all of his Angels. 'We will have to make many uneasy alliances today. The end is in sight, but we must strike swiftly and fiercely. We cannot achieve victory by ourselves. Deals must be struck with people who have been our foes in the past. Mr Dowling has always been our main target, the force we must defeat if we're to ultimately triumph over evil. His downfall is within our grasp, but only if we unite with other enemies of his.'

The Angels frown and murmur among themselves. Dr Oystein gives them a few moments to air their doubts, judging their mood perfectly, ever the skilled manipulator. In the end he raises a hand for calm.

'I must beg you to trust me,' he says with fake, sickening earnestness. 'I have sought your blind obedience before, but this is the last time I shall request it. I hate asking so much of you while revealing so little, but if we defeat Mr Dowling's dark forces today, I'll be completely open with you from this point on. The time for secrecy will have passed, and I'll be heartily glad to see it go.'

The Angels start muttering again, but with excitement this time.

'You think we can defeat Mr Dowling *today*?' Ashtat asks sceptically.

'Yes,' Dr Oystein says firmly. 'B has gone through hell, but emerged to lead us forward. She wavered in the brewery when we went to collect her yesterday, for reasons which I'll reveal later. But now she's back on our side. She knows where Mr Dowling's base is, and she can lead us to him. Also, she has rid him of his greatest weapon. He no longer possesses his vial of Schlesinger-10.'

There are cheers and some of the Angels swarm forward to embrace the doc and me, giving Rage, Owl Man and his dog a wide berth. Not all of them have been told about Schlesinger-10 and Clements-13, but those in the know quickly fill in the others, telling them that Schlesinger-10 is a virus that can wipe out all human survivors, that Mr Dowling has had it in his possession for many years, that we were never able to directly attack him in case he made good on his threat to uncork the vial. The cheering increases and the others crowd in around the beaming Dr Oystein. It's like we're celebrating at midnight on New Year's Eve.

Of course, it's all lies. The doc is the one who wants to use Schlesinger-10, to wipe out the last of the living. Owl Man's gagging order is driving me insane. I want to scream, warn them about their beloved doctor, tell them not to believe a bloody word he says. But my lips are sealed. I can only stand in the middle of the crowd and grimace, a muted dummy in the hands of my owlish master.

Having secured the backing he needs, Dr Oystein

dismisses his Angels, telling them to return to their rooms and make ready for battle. He says that Master Zhang will send for each of them in turn, to issue them with weapons and instructions. As they set off for their quarters, buzzing and babbling, he looks at them with genuine sadness.

'Not all of them will survive the coming battle,' he sighs. 'I'll grieve for each one who falls. But we must push on and accept our losses. It has always been so.'

Shrugging off his apparent unease, he departs to his own chambers to organise things ahead of the final push. Rage heads off after the doc, whistling merrily.

'This *is* for the best,' Owl Man says when we're alone. 'My uncle wants only what is good for this poor, tormented world. I know it doesn't seem that way to you, but future generations will look back on this time as an essential period of revolution. Today's living humans will be to them as our ape-like ancestors are to us. Evolution is all about those who rise to the top, not those who fall by the wayside.'

He gazes at me solemnly, awaiting my response. When I'm silent, he remembers that I'm mute because of his command and he chuckles. 'My apologies. You may speak now, Becky.'

'You're wrong,' I spit, with built-up fury. 'The apes weren't wiped out. They gave way naturally to our kind over millions of years. There's nothing natural about what you two are planning. You're playing God and nobody will thank you for that, any more than they thanked the Nazis when they tried to shape the world in *their* image.'

'We are nothing like the Nazis,' Owl Man snaps.

'No,' I agree. 'You're worse.'

He looks troubled by that accusation. He considers a retort, then shakes his head and lets it slide.

'It's a moot point,' he mutters. 'The die has been cast. Perhaps you're right. Maybe historians will look on us as monsters who interfered when they shouldn't have. But there is no pulling back from the precipice now. All we can do at this stage is jump and pray that we are the creatures of flight that we believe ourselves to be.

'Come,' he says wearily. 'Let's find a room for you and get you settled down. We have a busy night ahead of us. The world is about to end. We need to freshen up ahead of the catastrophic climax.'

ELEVEN

Owl Man sticks me in one of the complex's many free apartments. Before he goes, he tells me that I don't have to stay close to him any more – I'd automatically follow him otherwise – not to leave the flat until summoned, not to harm myself or anybody else, and not to say anything about what I've learnt over the last twenty-four hours to anyone who might pay me a visit. Then he clicks his tongue at Sakarias and off they trot.

I should probably prowl the confines of the rooms like a caged tiger, plotting and scheming, but I'm too tired for anything like that. So I lie on the bed and stare at the ceiling, letting my weary limbs relax, while trying not to think at all.

After a few hours, there's a knock on the door. I think about not replying or shouting at whoever it is to get lost, but I want to know who's there, so I call out gruffly, 'You don't need to knock. I'm a prisoner here. Just come in if you're bloody coming.'

The door opens and Ashtat, Shane and Carl slink into my bedroom. The three stand at the bottom of my bed and take their time studying me.

'You *have* been in the wars,' Ashtat finally notes.

'There's an understatement,' I grunt, and she smiles, relieved to see that I'm still as grumpy as I was before.

'Who did this to you?' Carl asks, nodding at my injuries. 'Mr Dowling?'

'No. Most of it was the work of Dan-Dan, but the babies tore me up too, when I got on the wrong side of them for a while.'

'You poor thing,' Ashtat says.

'Less of it,' I snap. 'I'm not looking for sympathy.'

'Just as well,' Shane snickers. 'We never liked you much anyway.'

I flip him the finger and we grin at each other. I start to relax, remembering what life was like when these guys were my room-mates and friends.

'Want to tell us about it?' Carl asks, sitting on the bed.

'Not really,' I sniff. Of course that's a lie. I'd love to tell them *everything* that has happened, but since I'm under a restraining order, I figure it's easier to ignore the recent past completely, rather than clam up every time I come close to a taboo revelation, like a malfunctioning ventriloquist's dummy.

'Can we get you anything?' Ashtat wants to know. 'Brains? Fresh bandages?'

'I'm good. I ate last night.'

There's a short silence. Nobody's sure what to say next.

'So,' I croak, stretching my arms and pretending to crack my knuckles. 'What have I missed?'

They smile and fill me in. They tell me how upset

the doc was when he found out that I'd trailed Rage and the others to County Hall, his anger at hearing the news of Rage's treachery and the deaths of Pearse and Conall. Many of the Angels wanted to go on the attack and rescue me, but he told them to bide their time. They weren't strong enough to target a fortress like Battersea Power Station, to take on the combined might of the KKK, the army and the members of the Board. The doc said they had to wait, hope and pray.

'Pray!' I jeer, shaking my head with disgust.

The others stare at me oddly. I want to tell them about the doc's warped pact with God, and exactly where his prayers have led us. But I'm under Owl Man's spell. Even if I wasn't, I'm not sure I'd spill the beans. I don't want to be the one who robs them of their faith in Dr Oystein. I know from experience how much that hurts.

The Angels searched the old Power Station after Mr Dowling and his mutant army had swept through it and moved on. They escorted the survivors to safety, mostly those who'd been held captive, though they helped some of the Klanners too.

'I wanted to let the bastards rot,' Shane growls. 'After what they'd done, I would have happily strung them up, like we did in New Kirkham.'

'We didn't do that,' Carl reminds him. 'The people who lived there made that decision.'

'It is not our right to pass judgement on the living,' Ashtat nods.

'So you keep telling me,' Shane scowls. 'But I think there are some crimes that even a zombie is fit to judge. If I'd had my way . . .'

As Shane grumbles to himself, Carl and Ashtat tell me how Dr Oystein and Master Zhang decided to move most of the Angels out of County Hall. The doc told them that although my capture was a dark hour for us, it might work in our favour. Having been taken under Mr Dowling's wing, he hoped I'd find the killer clown's vial of Schlesinger-10 and slip away with it.

'I thought he was saying that just to keep our spirits up,' Ashtat says, 'but he has been proved right, as he usually is. I suppose he knew something that we did not.'

He sure did. Since Owl Man was reporting back to him, the doc knew that Mr Dowling was infatuated with me, that he wanted me to be his bride. He'd helped Owl Man prepare me for a sneaky mental attack on my husband. But I can't tell them any of that. My tongue twists on itself every time I try to form the words.

'The doc would have taken us all with him,' Carl says, 'but Master Zhang said it was important not to tip off Mr Dowling. We needed to leave some Angels behind, to make it look as if we were still based in County Hall. He asked for volunteers to remain, telling them there was a good chance that Mr Dowling would attack and slaughter everyone.'

'Almost all of us offered to stay,' Shane says proudly. 'In the end we drew straws. At the time I wanted to draw one of the short straws, so that I could tackle the clown when he struck. But now I'm glad I didn't. We're going to get another shot at him, and this time we'll hit him where it hurts.'

'Maybe you'll be the one who wrings his neck,' Carl smirks.

'Maybe,' Shane says seriously, unaware that Carl is teasing him.

I smile at the trio and we spend the next half-hour chatting about ordinary stuff, like what they've been up to in my absence. Ashtat has been hard at work on a model of the Bow Quarter – she makes replicas out of matchsticks, so the ex-factory, where they once manufactured matches, seemed like an especially appropriate subject – while Carl and Shane have been scouring the boutique stores of the East End, Shane in search of flashy jewellery, Carl looking to replace the designer gear he had to leave behind in County Hall.

I cherish my short time with my friends, knowing this will probably be the last chance I get to shoot the breeze with them. I rarely appreciated our downtime before. Like the others, I was always looking forward to adventure, and taking the battle to Mr Dowling. I thought that hanging around was boring.

Now I see it for the gift that it was. This is a hard world. Adventure comes at a cost. The quiet moments are gold. Idly discussing a TV show or a band, gently bitching about people you don't like, or just sitting on a bed and staring out of a window while a friend sits by you and stares too . . .

Those are the best moments.

But I can't explain that to Ashtat, Carl and Shane. They wouldn't believe me. I don't think anyone ever realises how wonderful ordinary life is until something bad happens to them and they can't get back what they've lost.

I want to carry on chatting, but my ex-room-mates have to leave. There's a war to prepare for. They can't sit here gossiping all day. I'd like to tell them to get out, go to New Kirkham or somewhere like that, forget about the battle with Mr Dowling. But I'd be wasting my breath. Or whatever it is that passes for breath when you're a zombie.

So I say nothing as they file out, only watch silently, sadly, and wearily offer up a prayer, for whatever it's worth, asking God to go easier on them than He did on me.

Then I lie back, stare at the ceiling again, and wait.

TWELVE

I'm expecting to be here a long time, but to my surprise Rage turns up about an hour after my other old room-mates have departed. He doesn't bother knocking, just pushes straight in and grins lazily at me. 'Time to get your arse in gear.'

'Leave with you?' I snort. 'I don't think so.'

'Owl Man sent me,' he says. 'You're to consider yourself summoned.'

I get up and follow Rage to the door. I pause when I get there and stare at the space beyond. I try to step through, but my feet won't move. Rage watches me with a sly smirk.

'Try taking baby steps,' he says.

'Get stuffed,' I grunt, then shake my head. 'This is useless. I can't leave.'

Rage's smile widens. He spreads his arms like a magician and says in a deep voice, 'Alakazam, alaka-zoo, Becky Smith, come on through.'

I try again, but it's like there's an invisible barrier between me and the corridor.

'This is stupid,' I spit, taking a step back. 'You're just messing with me.'

'Yeah,' Rage chuckles, then his smile fades. 'But I'm not any more. *The truth is in the eyes.*'

'What does that mean?' I frown.

'It means I'm saying it's OK for you to leave the room now.'

I stare at Rage suspiciously, not wanting to be taken for a fool again.

'Seriously this time,' he says. 'Trust me.'

'Never,' I reply automatically, but take a couple of steps forward regardless, and this time I cross the threshold without any problems.

'Told you so,' Rage says smugly.

I scratch my head. 'How did you do that?'

He shrugs. 'The words are a control mechanism. They put you under the thumb of the person who says them.' He turns and thrusts his bum in my direction. 'Get down on your knees and kiss it, Becky.'

For a horrified second I think I'm going to be compelled to obey his command, but the urge to kneel doesn't take me. 'Up yours,' I retort with relief.

Rage laughs. 'Owl Man told me I wouldn't be able to manipulate you the way he can, but I thought I'd give it a go. He said I can't use the phrase to pull your strings, only counter an order that he's already given.'

'Any order?' I ask.

'I guess so,' Rage says.

'Let's try it,' I smile. 'Tell me I'm in complete control of myself again, and we'll see what happens.'

Rage laughs. 'You wish! No, you'd knock me out and take off. We're not letting you slip through our fingers that easily. Owl Man's been a lot of fun to work for. We have a beautiful relationship. I don't want to ruin it.'

'Seems like he doesn't trust you as much as you trust him though,' I sneer.

'What are you talking about?' Rage huffs.

I nod at the corner of a building across the way. Sakarias is there, watching us intently.

'Owly sent his dog to keep an eye on you,' I chuckle.

Rage's face darkens. Then he sniffs. 'I don't blame him. I wouldn't trust me too much either in his shoes.'

'How does it feel, having a lower place in the pecking order than a dog?' I ask, looking to wind him up.

'Doesn't bother me in the slightest,' Rage says. 'It's a dog-eat-dog world, so as long as the hound doesn't attack me, I'm happy to be its second. I'll even snap it a salute and call it *sir* if Owl Man tells me to.'

'Brown nose,' I grumble.

'And loving the smell,' he laughs and leads me on.

I try to strike the back of his head, hatching wild plans of killing him, then dealing with Sakarias – even though I know I wouldn't stand a chance against the mutant dog – and fleeing. But my hand won't rise. I'm still under orders not to hit anyone. Rage hasn't countermanded that instruction.

I could simply turn and run, but I wouldn't get very far — there are too many people around. If I try to break free, Owl Man might place even more restrictions on me. Better to wait until the odds are in my favour before I make my move.

I notice lots of new faces as we're working our way through the cluster of buildings. Most are soldiers, but there are some Klanners among them too. I stiffen when I spot the creeps in the white robes and hoods.

'I know,' Rage growls. 'I hate them too. I don't draw many lines – my motto's live and let live – but those sons of bitches are an exception.'

'Why side with them then?' I ask.

'Nothing to do with me,' he says. 'Your beloved Dr Oystein dealt them in. If such a wise and peaceful man wants to party with the Ku Klux Klan, who am I to disagree?'

I scowl at Rage, still wanting to stick up for the

doc somehow, despite all that he has done and is planning.

'Dr Oystein needs their help to overcome Mr Dowling,' Rage says softly as we pass through the ranks of soldiers and Klanners. 'I bet he hasn't told them what he's got lined up if they win. They wouldn't be so eager to pledge themselves to his cause if they knew that he was setting all of the living up for extinction.'

'We'd really throw the cat among the pigeons if we told them,' I mutter.

Rage nods. 'I thought about that. I was chatting with Ingrid earlier – she's not as fond of me as she used to be, not after the Pearse and Conall incident, but she was prepared to listen to my side of the story – and I thought about filling her in and letting her tell the others. But, as sweet as that would be, it will be even sweeter if we proceed as planned. I want to see the crazy Dowling brothers square off against one another.'

We come to a set of stairs and trot up three flights to an ordinary room. There's no sign that this is a command hub, except for the people present. Dr Oystein and Owl Man are there, along with Master Zhang and Reilly. A few army officers are also in attendance. I know one of them, Josh Massoglia, a captor of mine from way back. He winks in a friendly way when he sees me, but I blank him and focus on the final pair, a man and woman. The man is in KKK robes, though he's removed the hood. The woman is wearing a sharp, stylish business suit.

Justin Bazini and Vicky Wedge.

'I thought you two were dead,' I snap at the smiling members of the now-defunct Board.

'You wrote us off too soon,' the billionaire Bazini says smoothly. 'It was a close call, but we evaded Mr Dowling's dread troops. You know what we're like, Miss Smith — we always have a bolt-hole.'

'Disappointed to see us?' Vicky Wedge smirks. She used to be a right-wing politician. My dad thought she was fabulous.

'Not at all,' I smile. 'This way I'll hopefully get to see both of you die. I'm keeping my fingers crossed that it will be slow and horrible.'

Justin and Vicky laugh but Dr Oystein doesn't. He looks at me sadly, as if he's ashamed of the company he's been forced to keep. The odd thing is, I think he really does feel uncomfortable having to strike a deal with scum like this. The doc would rather do things his own way, without having to rely on the power-mad likes of Justin Bazini and Vicky Wedge. But he's a realist. He knows that sometimes he has to sell his soul in order to proceed. It's a price he's willing to pay, convinced as he is that God is asking it of him.

'Good to see you again, Becky,' Josh says.

'I can't say the same,' I toss back.

The soldier who was once my prison warden pulls a face. 'Don't forget that I set you free all those months ago. I could have torched you along with the rest of the zom heads.'

'I wish you had,' I mumble.

Josh sighs. 'Sometimes it's not worth doing a good deed for someone.'

'It is time to return to business, gentlemen,' Dr Oystein says. 'Let's not lose our focus.'

'No fear of that,' Josh says. 'I'm focused like a hawk.'

'As are we all,' Justin agrees. 'So tell us the plan, Oystein. You can't call us here like this and then leave us hanging.'

Dr Oystein shrugs. 'Like I told you, with B's aid I can find Mr Dowling's base. I had an idea where it was, but we were never able to target him because of the vial of Schlesinger-10 which he possessed.'

'And now he doesn't have that,' Josh nods. 'Yeah, you said. But you also said that Becky asked one of the babies to hide it. What if the clown has found it or if the baby didn't do what Becky told it to?'

Dr Oystein shrugs. 'If Mr Dowling has it, we'll try to wrest it from him. If we fail, and he looks as if he's going to open it, we will have to retreat.'

'We'll lose an awful lot of men,' one of the officers notes.

'Oh, please,' Vicky snorts. 'Nobody here is worried about them.'

'Speak for yourself,' the officer says angrily. 'I care about my troops.'

'More fool you,' Vicky says sweetly and turns her back on the seething soldier. 'So the girl leads us to the clown's base. We follow and engage the mutant enemy. What then?'

'It depends,' Dr Oystein replies. 'If Albrecht has recovered the vial and threatens us with it, we'll have to flee and plot afresh. Otherwise we'll fight on and kill him.'

'You're happy for us to execute him, despite the fact that he's your brother?' Josh asks.

'I will grieve for Albrecht if we succeed,' the doc says, sharing a dark look with the equally grim-faced Owl Man. 'But we cannot let him live. I am prepared to sacrifice him. There is no other way.'

'You're a cold fish,' Justin says. Then he grins. 'That's why I'm warming to you.'

'We must also look for the baby who hid the vial,' Master Zhang says, speaking for the first time. 'We do not fully understand the mindset of the babies. Even if we did, this one seems to act in a different manner to the others, according to the reports.'

'Yes,' Owl Man nods. 'Holy Moly is an unusual specimen. Maybe it is a result of the hole in its head, but it seems to be more of an individual than the rest of the infants.'

'Even if the baby did as B asked,' Dr Oystein continues, 'there is a chance that it will seek to recover the vial if it thinks we are poised to overcome the mutants. It might return the vial to Albrecht in that case, so that he can force us back. We must search for the child and either neutralise it or convince it to give us the vial.'

Justin frowns. 'You think we can do that?'

'The babies look upon Becky as their mother,' Owl Man says. 'They love her unconditionally. Holy Moly will listen to her. *If* we can find it.'

'What about the other babies?' Josh growls. 'The vicious little beasts tore us apart in Battersea. What makes you think we'll fare more favourably this time?'

'They had the element of surprise on their side before,' Master Zhang says. 'Now that your men know what to expect, they should be better prepared.

Also, the babies will be in a defensive rather than an offensive position. That changes things considerably.'

'Even so,' Josh says, 'I don't fancy our chances, not having seen the mini monsters in action.'

'Remember, we don't have to kill them all,' Owl Man says. 'We only need to find Albrecht. If we can remove him from the equation, the babies will fall under our control. Then you will only have the mutants to deal with, and I suspect many of them will switch sides if their leader is toppled.'

Josh is sceptical. 'You really think you can control the babies?'

'*We* can't,' Dr Oystein says softly. 'But *B* can. She is their mother. They crave the love and affection of a parental figure. If Albrecht is not there to fill that role, they will transfer all of their love and loyalty to her, and she can convince them to accept us as their foster-parents.'

'You trust her to cooperate?' Justin asks dubiously.

'Oh yes,' Owl Man answers, smiling slyly. 'Becky will do anything we ask. She is under my direct control, so she cannot deny me.'

Justin studies me closely. 'Interesting,' he purrs. 'Maybe I'll ask for some personal time with her when we're done with this business. I learnt quite a few things from Dan-Dan during our long days and nights together. Perhaps I'll try to revive his legacy.'

As I glare at the smirking billionaire, he slams his hands together and bellows at the others in the room, asserting his authority. 'Enough of the chit-chat. It's time to go to war. Let's get this show on the road!'

THIRTEEN

We roll out, several hundred soldiers, Klanners and Angels, with a few civilians added to the mix for good effect.

Ciara remains behind with the twins to keep the home fires burning. Cian and Awnya arc mad as hell that they're missing out on the action. They glare after us as we stream through the open gates. Dr Oystein stops to say something to them and they don't look quite so unhappy when he moves on. He must have told them they were doing an important job here, something like that. The doc is great at finding the right words to calm a person down. The best I've ever met.

We march through the streets as quietly as we can, Whitechapel Tube station our destination. A lot of zombies spot us as we pass and come roaring out to feast on the fresh brains of the living, lured from their shelters, despite the rays of the sun. Our troops deal with them casually, the Angels tackling and dispatching most of the assailants, the soldiers finishing off the few who slip through their undead, protective net.

Owl Man quizzes me as we proceed, milking me for information about Mr Dowling's base, where it is, the entrance, the layout. Even though he's been there many times, he's always been blindfolded well away from the base and led there by mutants, who've pushed him in a cart some of the way to further disorient him. He passes along the details to the other key players as I reveal them, and a hasty plan is knocked together while we walk.

He hasn't said anything about me having to stick close to him. I think it's slipped his mind. But it

certainly hasn't slipped mine. I can't escape in the middle of this lot, but I'm watching for an opportunity, waiting for the right moment. In the meantime I act like an obedient little puppy, hoping Owl Man won't think about making me do his bidding if I appear to be playing along voluntarily.

Justin Bazini and Vicky Wedge are accompanying us on our trek. I'm surprised they're part of the hunting party. I thought they'd secrete themselves somewhere safe and watch on a video feed from afar. Maybe they've grown tired of the passive life and want to dirty their hands.

The humans are nervous. An air of tension hangs so thickly about them that it's almost a fog. But nobody forced them to come. They're here because they want to fight for the future of their species and be part of the force that strikes the decisive blow, vanquishes Mr Dowling and secures control for the living.

At least that's what they think. They'd be even more nervous if they knew Dr Oystein was planning to double-cross them, that Mr Dowling was actually humanity's best hope of survival. If the doc kills him and forces me to bend the babies to his will, he'll tell Holy Moly to fetch the vial of human-eradicating Schlesinger-10, then turn it on those who think of him as an ally. He'll show no loyalty to these brave men and women. They'll die with all the rest of the living.

He could assist them if he wanted, turn them into mutants before uncorking the vial. He'll have unlimited access to Mr Dowling's secrets once the clown has been eliminated. He could create his own army of mutants out of these soldiers and Klanners, a reward for the humans who helped him realise his goals.

But he won't. He wants the adults out of the way. The removal of an entire generation. No one left to pass on bad habits to the babies.

I'm still being grilled by Owl Man when we arrive at the Tube station, and he carries on quizzing me as Dr Oystein's Angels, under the command of Master Zhang, push ahead to clear the area of reviveds. They operate swiftly and mercilessly, and soon the screams of dozens of zombies are echoing out to us.

Many of the humans shiver but nobody breaks away. Josh Massoglia and Justin Bazini chose their troops well. Everyone here is in the fight to the bitter end.

Eventually it goes quiet. There are a few grunts and shouts over the next few minutes as the Angels flush out any stragglers and finish them off. Then Master Zhang emerges. He looks grim, but that's nothing new, just his normal expression.

'The area is ours,' Zhang reports to Dr Oystein. 'There were four mutants on watch. We killed three of them. The other got away.'

'Then they'll know that we're coming.' Dr Oystein sighs. 'That is unfortunate but hardly unexpected.'

'Did you manage to question any of the mutants before you killed them?' Owl Man asks.

'Yes,' Zhang says. 'One of them confirmed that the clown was back in residence. Mr Dowling returned with a heavy heart after your message was passed on to him. He's waiting there for you.'

'And I'm coming as promised,' Owl Man says.

'Just bringing a few unexpected friends with you,' Justin Bazini laughs. 'He won't react too happily when he finds out that you've been deceiving him all this time. I'm glad I won't be with you, gentlemen. I think this will prove rather a bloody battle.'

'You're backing out?' I ask.

'Of course. Did you think I'd risk my life on such a dicey venture? No, I'm not interested in sacrificing myself for the greater cause. I simply came this far to oversee things and be part of the push for victory. You were so focused on what lies ahead that you probably missed my official photographer.'

Justin points to a cameraman who is standing on the roof of a car and taking photos of us.

'He's been trotting along, snapping away to his heart's content,' Justin beams. 'I'll go through the shots later and pick those I want to preserve for posterity.'

'So where are you heading now?' I ask. 'Back to the Bow Quarter?'

'No,' he says. 'I'll return to the headquarters where

I based myself after the fall of Battersea Power Station, sip some champagne and follow the conflict live — lots of my soldiers have video cameras attached to their helmets.'

I grin mockingly. 'An armchair voyeur. I thought you'd changed when I saw you marching along, that you'd grown a pair of *cojones*.'

'Oh, I have a very fine pair of *cojones*,' Bazini says calmly. 'I just don't feel the need to put them on the chopping block.'

As he's saying that, a small helicopter buzzes into view overhead. It sets down close to where we're standing, in a circle hastily cleared by Bazini's soldiers.

'My carriage awaits,' Bazini says, waving at me loftily.

'Splendid,' Vicky beams, stepping forward with him. 'I adore helicopters.'

Justin clears his throat. 'You weren't listening, my dear. I said *my* carriage awaits. Not *our*.'

Vicky stares at him, shaken. 'You're not taking me with you?' she squeaks.

'I need you here,' he says, offering her his most shark-like political smile. 'You must be my eyes and ears on the ground. I want you to work with the others and ensure they keep in line with our wishes.'

'But it's going to be a bloodbath,' Vicky shrieks. 'Most of the people going down there won't survive. I'll be as open to attack as the rest of them.'

Justin beams mercilessly. 'Then you'll have to pray that luck is with you.' His smile fades. 'You've served me admirably, and I hope this isn't the end of the road for us. But I want you to stay and convey my orders to the troops. This is important and I know you won't let me down. You've never disobeyed a request of mine in the past. You know better.'

Vicky gulps. Her lower lip trembles. If she wasn't a cold-hearted, racist bitch, I might feel sorry for her. Finally, under Justin's challenging gaze, she manages a weak smile and croaks, 'Of course I'll stay, if that's what you want.'

'Excellent.' He kisses her cheek, pinches her bum and heads for the waiting helicopter, swaggering like the foul god of war that he is.

'Bazini,' I call to him. 'If I never see you again, it'll be too soon.'

'The feeling, beastly girl, is mutual,' he trills. Then he trots to the chopper, hops in and takes off, sparing neither a gesture nor a thought for those he's left behind.

'His days are numbered,' Owl Man murmurs in my ear.

'Good,' I grunt. 'If all of the human race has to fall in order for the likes of him to be taken down, I guess it's an almost acceptable trade-off.'

I share a wry smile with Owl Man. Then Josh Massoglia blows a whistle and calls to the assembled troops.

We advance.

FOURTEEN

We head along the tracks until one of the team finds the panel that I told Owl Man about. It's cleverly disguised to look like just another part of a standard wall. If you weren't looking for it, you'd never notice it.

A couple of engineers dismantle the panel to reveal the low, narrow tunnel beyond. Josh steps forward and nods for me to join him. We stare into the gloom.

'Even smaller and tighter than you led us to believe,' Josh mutters. 'And you say there's a maze of tunnels like this one?'

'Yeah.'

'You'll be able to find your way through it?'

I nod. 'I wasn't paying much attention when the babies brought me this way, but Mr Dowling has mental maps of all the tunnels and I copied those over when I bonded with him.'

'And you think it took about half an hour to make it to the clown's lair?' Josh presses.

'Yeah.'

Josh rubs his chin unhappily. 'We'll be vulnerable. The tunnel's just a couple of metres high, maybe less in places from what I can see of it. Many of my people will have to advance in a crouch.'

'You should have hired Munchkins for the job,' Rage jokes.

'Are you having second thoughts?' Dr Oystein asks.

'No,' Josh sighs. 'It's too late for those. I'm just saying it's going to be hard. I've a bad feeling about this. Maybe we can send a small team ahead with Becky to check that the way is clear before the rest of us follow.'

'We have no time for that,' Zhang snaps. 'Dowling knows we are coming. We must strike swiftly, before he can organise his forces.'

'Besides, you would be equally vulnerable here,' Dr Oystein adds. 'Albrecht might have set explosives in the roof above us. He could bring it crashing down on your heads at any given moment.'

Josh looks up sharply. 'If he's wired this one, he might have wired the roofs of the tunnels too.'

'Perhaps,' the doc says. 'I do not think he will risk killing me by bringing them down – he finds the world a more interesting place with me in it to plot and battle against – but if he is more desperate than I imagine . . .'

Josh curses, then forces a shaky smile. 'What the hell. Let's push on. Take the lead, Becky. We'll be close behind.'

I move into the tunnel, flanked by Dr Oystein and Owl Man, Sakarias and Rage just behind us. We proceed in a straight line until we come to the first branch. I stop and stare, waiting for Mr Dowling's memories to snap into place.

'Make sure you take the correct turn,' Owl Man whispers. 'At this and every other junction. Do not lead us astray.'

'The thought never crossed my mind,' I lie, because of course it had. But now that Owl Man has commanded me to follow the right path, the chance to strand them in the tunnels is lost. Although, having said that, he still hasn't ordered me to stay close by his side, so I cling to the desperate hope that I can slip free at some point.

As the map forms inside my head, I find myself turning left. I try to fight it and turn right, to lead my captors a merry dance, but Owl Man's hold over me is too great.

We progress, an army at my heels, me up front guiding them, a puppet in Owl Man's hands, the figurehead on the prow of the good ship *Destruction*.

FIFTEEN

We make slow progress, shuffling along, stretched thinly, with barely room for the troops to march three abreast. They're sweating, grumbling, twitchy. They didn't expect it to be this claustrophobic. Apart from a few lights, it's as dark as a mine. The soldiers have torches, but they've been told not to light them, since we don't want to draw attention to ourselves.

Despite our attempts at stealth, everyone knows it's only a matter of time until we're attacked, and the assault finally comes when we're deep into the maze, far from the exit.

I don't see our assailants – they strike further back down the line – but I hear the screams as humans are targeted by mutants or babies. Scattered gunfire. More screams.

'What's happening?' Josh bellows, and one of his soldiers comes pushing through the crowd to report.

'They're hitting us from smaller side tunnels,' the soldier gasps. 'Pulling us away one at a time. Dragging the victims off into the darkness.'

'Tell everyone to bunch up and stand back to back,' Josh snaps. 'Open fire if they hear footsteps or see anything. Those with bayonets should hold them close to the ground — the babies come in low.'

There are more screams as we nudge ahead even slower than before. I glance back and see blood spurting into the air, hitting the ceiling, dripping back on to the heads of those still alive.

As I'm watching, a mutant's head and shoulders appear out of the ceiling. There must be vertical

shafts up there, like chimneys. The mutant grabs a soldier by her head and twists, snapping the woman's neck. Another soldier turns and fires, but the mutant has already withdrawn, laughing hysterically.

Sakarias barks and I look ahead. I spot a line of babies, their eyes glowing red.

'If they attack you – or if anyone else tries to harm you – defend yourself,' Owl Man says commandingly. 'Fight to the bitter end.'

'Don't I always?' I mutter sourly, but Owl Man need not have worried. Though the babies stream towards us seconds later, they dash through my legs, and the legs of those close to me, and target the soldiers and Angels behind us, fangs snapping left and right, spreading fear and pain in a swift, miniature tsunami.

We struggle on while under siege, the soldiers fighting back as best they can, crawling over the bodies of the dead and wounded, doggedly following Owl Man and me as we shuffle along unchallenged.

I walk in a dazed state, trying to drown out the

screams, taking turns through the maze when I feel that I should. Owl Man stays by my side, whispering to me, keeping me in line, gently urging me on.

I lose track of time. It feels like we've been down here forever. The babies made it to the base in half an hour when they were carrying me, but even bearing my weight they were able to clip along at a fair speed, whereas we've been reduced to a punishing, blood-drenched crawl.

I take a right and we move down a short tunnel which opens out into a cavern. It feels vast after the tight confines of the maze. The soldiers spill into it gratefully and gather at the centre, forming a defensive ring.

'This feels like a trap,' Master Zhang mutters, squinting at several lights set in the walls, illuminating the area brightly.

'Yeah,' Josh pants, looking worried. 'But we need a break. My troops have to regroup and sort themselves out. We can use the time to take stock and figure out how many we've lost.'

'That is irrelevant,' Dr Oystein says. 'We should press on. Any pause plays into their hand, not ours.'

'Maybe,' Josh sniffs. 'But this lot will crumble if we push them on too soon. It was hell coming through the tunnels. They're not undead like you. They're only human. They need a rest.'

Dr Oystein snorts impatiently, but trusts Josh's understanding of his men and women. He says nothing more, waiting for Josh to give the word.

The soldiers and Klanners are packed into the cramped cave, forming a dense circle around us. There's room for all, but only just, and there wouldn't have been if we hadn't lost so many of our forces in the tunnels.

The attacks cease. The mutants and babies withdraw. We hear the mutants chuckling and catcalling, blowing whistles to set our teeth on edge, but there's no sign of them.

Josh demands reports and his people respond quickly, listing injuries and losses. They're spooked by what we've been through, but they haven't cracked. They've lost friends and comrades, but they didn't expect anything different. These are seasoned pros. They won't give up.

Dr Oystein summons his Angels while the humans are settling back into shape. 'I want you all to move to the front when we advance again,' he says softly. 'We cannot afford to march so slowly this time. If the humans can't match our speed, we will leave them behind and fight the final battle by ourselves.'

'Are you counting me as one of them or one of you?' someone asks, and I spot a grinning Reilly near the back of the pack of Angels.

'One of them,' Dr Oystein says coldly to the ex-soldier who has helped shape us into a fighting force to be reckoned with. Then, as Reilly blinks nervously, the doc cracks a smile. 'Forgive me. I could not resist the chance to tease you. Even in our darkest moments, we must make room for a sliver of levity. You belong to us, of course, my friend. But you must keep up. We cannot make allowances for you.'

'No probs, doc,' Reilly says with relief. 'I want to be there. I wouldn't miss this for the world, not after all the time I've spent with you guys.'

'I'll look out for you and make sure you get home safely to Ciara,' Carl says confidently. 'It'll be like when we used to take you out training, when we needed a live guinea pig to stir up the reviveds.'

'That's comforting,' Reilly says drily. 'But if you don't mind, I'd rather –'

His next words are drowned out by a long, ferocious howl. All noise in the cavern ceases as everyone looks around nervously.

'What the hell was that?' Josh barks. 'Mutants? Babies?'

'No,' Owl Man says sombrely, looking genuinely worried. 'Worse than that, and most unexpected.'

As Josh stares at him, Owl Man points. We turn, and I spot a stream of people flooding into the cavern from tunnels dotted around the edges. The entrances had been blocked, so that they looked like parts of the walls. But now the obstructions have been removed and an army of vicious, bloodthirsty troops is flooding through. But, as Owl Man said, these aren't the mutants or babies that we thought we'd be facing down here.

They're zombies.

SIXTEEN

It's been a long time since I looked upon the walking dead as a genuine threat. They've been little more than a nuisance when I've been by myself or with other revitaliseds. I've had to be wary of them when I've travelled with living humans, but even then they've been easy enough to deal with. They're not as sharp, fast or smart as those of us with functioning brains. I'd started to take them for granted.

But they're far more menacing down here. We're trapped, the smell of hundreds of fresh brains drawing the zombies on. Nowhere to run, no way to repel them, no room to manoeuvre. Our weapons and expertise are of limited use. The soldiers at the edges can't fend off their attackers. Many are converted as they fall prey to the undead swarm, and they turn on their friends and allies, adding to the chaos.

Josh and the other commanders bellow orders. The troops do their best to obey, but the body count is mounting and it's clear that we're in serious trouble. Some soldiers try to flee and the group begins to fragment.

As the zombies rip into the flesh of the living, the mutants and babies push up behind them, taking advantage of any divisions, moving into the gaps which the zombies have created, isolating small pockets of soldiers and Klanners, finishing them off viciously and efficiently.

Lots of Angels dart to the aid of the humans. Dr Oystein and Master Zhang try to call them back, to hold us together, but it's turned noisy as hell and their voices are lost to the crazy din.

Vicky Wedge is standing close by Owl Man, cringing, weeping, wringing her hands. Justin must be barking something at her through the headset which she's wearing, because she forces her head up and starts moaning descriptions of what she's witnessing.

The group that I'm part of is protected from the attacks by the soldiers packed around us. Rage looks frustrated. He's on his toes, peeking over the heads of the humans, looking for someone to fight. 'Come on,' he mutters. 'Come on!'

Carl gets ready to leap to the aid of the struggling soldiers.

'No,' Ashtat stops him. 'Dr Oystein told us to stay.'

'But we can't just stand by and do nothing,' he cries.

'We'll be doing plenty soon,' Shane says, keeping his cool. 'Don't be in such a rush. They'll come to us. You won't have long to wait.'

More zombies stream into the cavern. The mutants must have rounded them up from one of the underground Tube stations, or perhaps they've been holding them in reserve for a day like this.

The newcomers throw themselves into the bloody, ragged mess, biting flesh, gouging eyes, ripping out tongues, digging through skulls into brains. It's been a long time since they got to feast like this. They're making the most of it.

'We must push on,' Master Zhang says.

'And leave my people behind?' Josh barks.

Zhang shrugs. 'They're finished. They have served their purpose, but can continue to be of value for a while longer. If we leave now, they will buy us valuable time. If we stay, we'll gain nothing and their sacrifice will have been a waste.'

Josh is wild-eyed. He gulps several times, trying to make up his mind.

'Justin says that we have to do what Dr Oystein tells us,' Vicky Wedge whimpers. 'He says the success of the mission is all that matters. Losses are acceptable. He . . .' She pauses, grimaces, then repeats what the absent billionaire is telling her. 'He says to stop acting like a child. You know what you have to do, so do it.'

'Easy for him to say,' Josh grumbles. 'He doesn't

have the blood of good men and women on his hands.' Then he sighs and looks to the doc for guidance.

'This way,' Dr Oystein says simply, and we push on, a small group of us, some of his Angels, Master Zhang, Owl Man, Rage and Sakarias, Josh and Reilly, Vicky Wedge, a unit of soldiers and a handful of Klanners, leaving the bulk of our forces behind to perish gruesomely at the hands of the marauding zombies.

SEVENTEEN

We hurry through the tunnels, able to move swiftly now that we're not part of a major assault force. Josh discusses tactics with Dr Oystein and Master Zhang as we run. He doesn't think there are enough of us to ensure victory if we manage to track down Mr Dowling.

'He'll have surrounded himself with scores of his best people,' Josh pants. 'Maybe he'll use another army of zombies as a shield. How are we going to break through when there are only a few dozen of us?'

'I do not think that we will encounter such an obstacle,' Dr Oystein says. 'This is personal. Albrecht will want to face us openly, on an equal footing. He knows that the moment of destiny has arrived. It is not in his nature to stack the odds against us in an effort to cheat fate.'

'I wish I shared your belief,' Josh says glumly.

Dr Oystein smiles thinly. 'Trust me. I know my brother. He'll want to defeat us, but in his own way, on his own terms.'

Josh shakes his head and starts to ask another question. He's cut short by Owl Man, who suddenly stops and raises a hand.

'What is it?' Master Zhang asks, drawing to a halt beside the tall freak.

'I thought I saw . . .' Owl Man murmurs.

'. . . a puddy tat?' Rage smirks.

'No,' Owl Man says seriously. 'A baby with a hole in its head.'

A mutant drops from a hidden niche in the ceiling and lashes out at one of the soldiers. Ashtat is close by. She karate-chops the mutant's throat and he falls to the floor, choking. There are no other movements or sounds.

Then I spot the baby peering round a corner. There's no mistaking that hole in its skull.

'Holy Moly,' I whisper.

The baby's face lights up and it steps forward. A soldier raises his rifle.

'At ease,' Owl Man says softly but firmly. He takes a step towards the baby. Sakarias advances with him.

'*big doggy mummy*,' Holy Moly squeaks. '*woof woof.*'

I smile shakily. 'Be careful. This doggy bites.'

'*holy moly bites too*,' the baby giggles, showing its tiny fangs.

'Tell it to –' Owl Man starts to say to me.

'Run, Holy Moly!' I shout before Owl Man can complete his order. 'Run now!'

'No!' Owl Man roars. 'Tell it to come back!'

My lips instantly start to move. 'Come –' I begin, but to my relief I see that I'm too late. The baby obeyed the instant I yelled, and took off like a startled rabbit.

Owl Man curses and hurries after the fleeing infant. The others follow and I'm dragged along with them, smiling at my small act of rebellion, hoping it will be enough to wreck their plans, but knowing that's a slim hope. Slimmer than an ice cube's hope in Hell.

EIGHTEEN

Holy Moly doesn't manage to shake us loose. The baby tears through the tunnels, but we keep it in our sights. Sometimes we even get close when it pauses to study some obscure outcrop of rock or other.

I think we're being toyed with. I know how fast the babies can run, and these tunnels are their playpen. Holy Moly could disappear within seconds if it truly wished to lose us. I've got a feeling we're being led into another trap.

I consider sharing my suspicions with Owl Man, but why bother? Apart from my friends, I don't care about any of this lot. Let them run into a pit full of stakes if that's what the baby has lined up. It would probably be for the best if they did. Get them all out of harm's way nice and swiftly. I'd die too, of course, but I've no problem with that, not if I can take the doc and his crew down with me.

There are occasional attacks from stray mutants or zombies, but nothing like the concentrated strikes that we had to endure on our way to the cavern. Most of our enemies seem to be massed round the doomed soldiers. Or else they're with Mr Dowling, waiting for us up ahead.

I expect Holy Moly to lead us to the clown's base, maybe even his personal chambers. I figure that's the sort of place where my unhinged husband will want to end this. But instead we veer away from the central part of the complex, down a series of tunnels which are new to me.

The others are worried. They think the baby might be leading us off into the middle of nowhere.

'Maybe it wants to protect Becky and steer her clear of the danger areas,' Owl Man says.

'Should we abandon the chase and focus on finding Albrecht?' Master Zhang asks.

'No,' Dr Oystein snaps. 'The baby knows where the vial is. If we can get hold of that, everything else is irrelevant. We will stick with the pursuit until we catch up with or lose sight of the child.'

The doc's excited. He senses victory. Owl Man looks as inscrutable as always. Hard to tell what he's thinking. Rage is chuckling softly at some personal joke and tapping the head of an axe which is hanging by his side. Everyone else looks nervous, even the normally cool Master Zhang.

We turn another corner and spot Holy Moly waiting for us. The baby puts a finger to its lips and makes a shushing noise. Then it starts to creep ahead.

Dr Oystein hurries after the baby. Owl Man reaches out to stop him. 'This is an unusual situation,' he murmurs. 'Are you sure you wish to proceed?'

'What choice do we have?' Dr Oystein replies.

'There is always a choice,' Owl Man says.

'No,' the doc retorts. 'In this case there isn't.'

We follow Holy Moly round a few more bends, no longer racing to catch up, taking it slowly, letting the baby guide us. The troops are readying their weapons, wiping blood or dirt from their foreheads and cheeks, preparing for battle.

Finally we come to a door. I spot Ivor pushing forward, looking interested — he gets a buzz when presented with a new kind of lock. But then Holy Moly jumps, grabs hold of the handle and pulls down, swinging in with the door as it opens, and Ivor sees that there's no lock to pick. He falls back, disappointed, as the baby lets go with a giggle and trots into a large chamber. As we enter, I see that the walls are painted with blood and excrement, and decorated with links of guts and limbs, the trademark interior design of the twisted Mr Dowling.

And there, at the centre of the room, stands the crazy clown. He's bent over a table, chewing a corner of a map, surrounded by mutants and babies. Kinslow is by his master's side, pointing to an area on the map, discussing something with his fellow mutants. Claudia, the girl whom Owl Man spared in

the pub in Wapping, is with them, though she isn't saying much.

Nobody spots us as we fan out. We thought this was a trap, but it looks like we aren't expected. I'm confused, and I can tell that Dr Oystein is too. Maybe our foes are only pretending to be unaware of us, to lull us into a false sense of security.

I keep waiting for the floor to open beneath us or nets to drop from overhead, but nothing happens. The mutants carry on their conversation as if we aren't there, and we study them incredulously, nobody wanting to be the first to break the bizarre spell.

Holy Moly bounds up to Mr Dowling and leaps on to his back. The clown pats the baby absent-mindedly and carries on chewing.

'*daddy,*' Holy Moly says.

Mr Dowling ignores it.

'*daddy,*' Holy Moly says again.

'Not now,' Kinslow says with surprising sweetness. 'Daddy's busy. He'll play with you later.'

'*but i brought mummy to see him,*' Holy Moly says, and the mutants fall silent.

Kinslow half-turns to stare at the beaming baby. 'What?'

'*holy moly brought mummy*,' the baby says, leaping from Mr Dowling's back to point at us.

Kinslow turns the rest of the way round, along with the other mutants. The babies swivel too, all at the same time, in their eerie, synchronised fashion. Mr Dowling is the last to look, reluctantly letting go of the map, spitting out a few pieces, then turning to smile at me crazily.

The mutants and babies stare at us. We stare back. Nobody says a word. The sense of shock is almost palpable.

Then Holy Moly cries out, '*mummy. daddy. kiss and make up.*'

NINETEEN

'Kiss and make up!' Kinslow cackles. 'That's a good one.'

'*Hello, my beloved,*' Mr Dowling whispers inside my head, ignoring his henchman, his soft, telepathic voice contrasting with his wildly rolling eyes and peeled-back lips. '*It is good to see you again, even if the circumstances are far from ideal.*'

'Hi, hubby,' I mutter. 'Sorry for ruining the wedding night.'

The clown laughs hysterically and claps loudly.

'Albrecht,' Dr Oystein says, stepping forward, and

Mr Dowling stops clapping. 'This does not have to end in tears. Let us reach a compromise. We do not need to shed blood here today.'

'*Why is he looking to compromise?*' Mr Dowling asks, his words only sounding inside my head. '*Didn't you give him the vial?*'

'Share nothing with him,' Owl Man murmurs in my ear before I can reply. I don't think he can eavesdrop on my conversation with Mr Dowling, but he can see that we're in contact. He doesn't want me to give the game away.

The clown cocks his head and stares at me when I don't answer his question. '*Your mind is not your own. Zachary has tinkered with it. I understand now why you attacked me. It was not your doing. I forgive you.*'

I smile warmly at that and turn to Owl Man. 'Let me speak with him. Please. I won't tell him anything about the vial.'

Owl Man exchanges a glance with Dr Oystein, who nods slowly.

'Very well,' Owl Man says. 'But reveal nothing of

our mission or what has happened to the sample of Schlesinger-10.'

I face Mr Dowling and open my thoughts to him. 'Sorry,' I say again, but this time without moving my lips. 'This wasn't something that I planned. I know how much you were prepared to sacrifice for me. I didn't mean to betray you before you had a chance to prove yourself.'

'Perhaps it was for the best,' Mr Dowling sighs as his mutants glare at us and growl softly. *'I don't think I could have made you happy. The heavens were set against us. It wasn't our time. But perhaps it can be, depending on how things play out today.'*

'I doubt it,' I tell him truthfully. 'Too much has happened. Besides, how could you trust me? You don't know what else Owl Man might have done to my brain. Even *I* don't know.'

'Clever little Zachary,' Mr Dowling says bitterly. *'I taught him too well.'*

The clown does a quick pirouette, catching everyone by surprise, then opens his mind to the rest of his followers, including Kinslow, who gives voice to his words for the benefit of those who haven't bonded with him.

'You did well to find me, Oystein. I didn't think you would track me down to my war room. I was going to face you in my personal chambers later, when I'd stripped you of all your followers and hopes.'

'This doesn't have to be a room of war,' Dr Oystein says, taking another step towards his estranged, deranged brother. 'It can be a room of peace. Let us build bridges, restore what we've destroyed, work with one another again, like we did in the past.'

'*There can be no going back,*' Mr Dowling transmits sadly, and Kinslow says it aloud for him.

'I'm not talking about going back,' Dr Oystein says. 'I want to move forward with you and Zachary by my side, to forge a new world. The three of us can be the architects of the future. We have come so far separately. Let's go the rest of the way hand in hand.'

'I wish that we could,' Mr Dowling says through Kinslow, 'but you and I crave different things.'

'We don't have to,' Dr Oystein presses. 'Zachary and I can work on your damaged brain and try to repair it. Trust us, Albrecht. Work with us. I'm your brother, Zachary is your son, and, despite all that we have been through, we've never stopped loving you. Let us help you, so that we can be a family again.'

Mr Dowling rubs the v-shaped grooves in his cheeks. Kinslow is looking at his master oddly, aggressively. The mutant has picked up a scythe. I think he might chop off the clown's head if he sides with Dr Oystein.

'*What do you think, children?*' Mr Dowling asks the babies, looking down upon his mini terrors. '*Would you like it if I kissed and made up?*'

'*with yummy mummy?*' the babies all ask together.

'*No, sillies,*' the clown chuckles. '*With Oystein.*'

The babies look blank. They don't care about the doc or anybody else. The question means nothing to them.

'If I grant you the support of my people,' Mr Dowling says softly through Kinslow, facing his brother again, 'what will you give me in return?'

'What do you want?' Dr Oystein asks eagerly, taking yet another step forward. He's almost within touching distance of the clown. Mr Dowling glances at Kinslow and shares a private thought with him.

'Will you return his vial of Schlesinger-10?' Kinslow says pleasantly.

'I can't,' Dr Oystein says. 'I don't know where . . .'

The doc stops, his face falling, as he realises he's been tricked.

'*I thought as much,*' Mr Dowling crows, his laughter echoing inside all of our heads. '*He doesn't have it. The vial has gone missing.*' Then, as Dr Oystein flounders, Mr Dowling throws his head back, waves imperiously at his followers, and screeches telepathically, '*Children — attack!*'

TWENTY

As the mutants and babies surge forward, Mr Dowling launches himself at Dr Oystein. The brothers fall to the floor, tearing and punching at one another.

Shane moves in on Kinslow as the mutant sweeps to the aid of his master. Kinslow spots the threat and swings his scythe. Shane ducks beneath the blade and slams his foot into the mutant's stomach. Kinslow's driven back with a winded cry.

Josh Massoglia and Reilly marshal the few human troops who made it through, roaring at them to aim carefully, not fire wildly, and choose their targets.

Master Zhang glides ahead, most of the Angels falling in behind him. As the mutants attack, he swats them aside, barely exerting himself, a lethal, tightly wound fighting machine.

Ashtat follows Shane and throws a few karate kicks at Kinslow, knocking him off his feet. He doesn't know what's hit him. Go, girl!

Vicky Wedge carries on a running commentary, telling Justin Bazini about the battle, adding words to the images which he's picking up from the various cameras scattered among his remaining soldiers. She looks white as a ghost, and flinches any time someone comes near, but she doesn't back off.

Carl springs about the room like a bionic bunny. This is his speciality. He comes down upon his foes from out of nowhere, thrusting them aside, breaking up groups, causing confusion.

The babies swarm towards me. I'm not sure if they plan to hug me or eat me. Before I can find out, Holy Moly throws itself between us and bellows at them, '*mummy.*'

The babies stop instantly and I'm reminded of the

power struggle in my wedding chamber, when they would have torn me apart if not for Holy Moly's intervention. This time it's easier for the idiosyncratic little baby to distract them.

'*lots more for us to kill,*' Holy Moly says, pointing at the soldiers and Angels. '*leave mummy and daddy alone.*'

'*yes,*' the babies say. '*we love mummy and daddy.*'

Then they hurl themselves at the humans. Lots of the babies are caught in the crossfire and blown apart, but there are so many of them that more push in to replace the casualties and they descend on the soldiers without slowing.

A few of the babies target Owl Man, who has been standing by my side, looking worried. As they attack, Sakarias bounds to his defence. The dog grabs one of the infants and shakes it like a doll, grinding through its ribcage, tearing it apart, letting its carcass drop.

The dead baby's comrades hiss and leap on to Sakarias's back. The dog snaps at them, then rolls over, trying to squash them. Owl Man leans down to pull them off, but one of the babies latches on to his hand and flashes its fangs. Owl Man yelps and jerks away. Two of his fingers have been ripped clean off. He stares at the bloody stumps, dumbfounded.

A pair of babies clamber on to Sakarias's exposed belly. As the shaggy sheepdog howls, they rip the lining of its stomach to shreds and burrow in. I stare with fascination as one of the babies crawls through the mutant canine's body and up its throat. I spot a hand shoot through the space at the back of the dog's mouth. Then the baby's fingers find Sakarias's brain and tear into it. Moments later the dog falls still and the light leaves its sad, soulful eyes.

I feel sorry for Sakarias. It didn't ask to become Owl Man's mutated pet. It was a friendly thing in its own fierce way. But there's no time to mourn a dead dog. Owl Man is still staring at his mutilated hand. This might be my chance to break free.

I spin round towards the exit, meaning to run and leave the fighting behind me. I jam my hands over my ears, to hopefully block out any commands that Owl Man might yell after me when he sees me taking off. My plan is to call to Holy Moly as I flee, ask the baby to join me, so that I can find out where it hid the vial of Schlesinger-10.

But Rage, standing next to me, has other ideas. As I swivel, he wraps his arms round me and murmurs, 'Going somewhere, Becky?'

'Let go, you bastard,' I shout, kicking out at him.

'Not a hope,' he grunts. 'This is the endgame. No one leaves before the fat lady sings.'

As I continue to kick at Rage, I spy Kinslow back on his feet. He lashes out blindly with his scythe and the tip burrows itself in the side of Ashtat's head. She steps away from the mutant, stunned, blood seeping from the wound, staining her otherwise pure-white headscarf.

Shane roars furiously and knocks Kinslow to the floor. He throws a series of punches at the mutant, cursing wildly. The girl from the pub, Claudia, tries to pull him away, but the furious Shane shrugs her aside and carries on punching.

'Ashtat,' I moan.

I don't know if she hears, but she turns towards me.

Rage had been chuckling, but he stops when he sees Ashtat.

'Poor cow,' he sighs.

Ashtat reaches towards us. The scythe is sticking out of her head, the handle quivering.

Somebody drops a gun, and Claudia kicks it across to Kinslow. I yell a warning to Shane, but Kinslow grabs the weapon before the Angel can react, jams it up under Shane's chin and fires. The gun snags on one of the chains which Shane always wears, throwing off Kinslow's aim, so, instead of tearing through the middle of Shane's head, the bullet explodes out behind his left ear. He falls to one side, screaming with pain, desperately trying to poke bits of his brain back into place.

Claudia laughs hysterically, picks up a few pieces of Shane's brain, and stuffs them into her mouth, pretending she likes the flavour. I wish now that Owl Man had killed her when he had the chance. If this is what comes of being merciful, I'll never show pity again.

Kinslow growls like a bear and Claudia spits out

the cranial pulp and helps him back to his feet. Without thanking her, he grabs the handle of the scythe and yanks it from Ashtat's head. She cries out once, then sinks and convulses, one of the undead no longer, at rest for all time.

The blonde, leather-clad Ingrid and quick-fingered Ivor have swept ahead of Master Zhang, finding a temporary gap and exploiting it. Having slipped through the net of bodies, they close in on the battling brothers at the eye of the storm. Dr Oystein and Mr Dowling are tearing at one another like a pair of rabid dogs, biting, scratching, ripping. Flesh hangs from them in strips, and each is coated in blood.

Ivor is just ahead of Ingrid, looking ready for business, but then a stray bullet hits the side of his head and he drops suddenly, an unmoving husk, and I know with a single glance that he'll never pick a lock again.

Ingrid roars vengefully but doesn't slow down. Ignoring her fallen friend, she grabs Mr Dowling, to tug him off her beloved doctor. The clown turns, smiles, opens his mouth and spits a stream of large ants into her eyes. Ingrid screams with alarm and flails sideways, slapping at the ants as they dig into her cheeks and target her eyes. They must be some breed of super ant, because they bite in hard, making it almost impossible for her to dislodge or squash them.

Reilly and Josh are standing near the rear of the remaining soldiers, still yelling orders. They're holding the team together, getting them to cover as many angles as possible. It's hard work staving off the lightning-fast babies, but they're coping.

Then a stray zombie lurches into the room through the door which we didn't think to shut behind us. It stumbles towards Josh. Reilly spots it, shouts a warning and shoves Josh aside. The zombie misses its target, but the bones sticking out of its fingers catch the flesh of Reilly's throat and tear softly into it.

Reilly curses and shoots the zombie through the head. It collapses in a heap. Reilly curses again, then presses his fingers to his throat. They come away wet and red. It's only a flesh wound, but, when you're one of the living and the wound is the work of a zombie, that's enough.

Reilly catches my eye and smiles miserably. 'If you see her, tell Ciara I love her,' he cries.

'She already knows,' I shout back.

Reilly salutes me, then presses the mouth of his gun to his own temple, closes his eyes and releases himself from the grip of the nightmare which would otherwise claim him whole.

Carl leaps through the air, lands beside us and winces. 'What a sickener. I had a lot of respect for Reilly.' He looks at me, still struggling and trying to break free, and asks Rage, 'What are we going to do with B now?'

'That's for Owl Man to decide,' Rage huffs. 'Hey, Owly, are you compos mentis or are you gonna go on staring at your fingers all day?'

Owl Man looks up, blinks dumbly, then smiles shakily. 'My apologies. I was not expecting this. It hurts. I had almost forgotten what real pain was like.'

'What about Becky?' Rage asks. 'What do you want her to do?'

Owl Man studies me for a moment, then nods. 'Call Holy Moly,' he tells me.

'Holy Moly,' I shout, having to obey.

The baby is close by, keeping an eye on me, and it runs across, beaming.

'Ask it where the vial is,' Owl Man says.

'Holy Moly,' I say softly, kneeling before the baby. 'Did you hide the vial like I asked you to?'

'*yes, mummy,*' Holy Moly says proudly.

'Where?' Owl Man barks.

'Where?' I repeat.

Holy Moly bares its teeth at Owl Man, not liking the tone he took with me.

'It's OK,' I soothe the baby. 'Don't worry about him. Where did you hide the vial?'

'*in a safe place,*' Holy Moly says. '*i'm clever like mummy and hid it where no one would think to look. do you want me to show you, mummy?*'

'Yes,' Owl Man gasps.

'Yes,' I'm forced to echo.

Holy Moly's smile spreads. Then it bends and shakes its head from side to side. At first I think the baby's having a fit. But then something glints inside the hole in its head. As we gawp, the baby reaches up, sticks a few fingers inside the wound in its skull, and gently eases out the vial of Schlesinger-10.

'*ta-dah,*' it exclaims.

TWENTY
-ONE

Rage has loosened his grip. His gaze is fixed on the vial of Schlesinger-10. It's such a powerful weapon that even the usually sneering Rage is reduced to a solemn, wide-eyed figure, thinking about all of the people who will die if the vial is uncorked and its toxic fumes released.

Carl is also staring at the vial, awestruck, as is Owl Man. The trio are momentarily frozen.

But I've no time for freezing. This is my chance. It hits me in an instant what I must do, how I can turn this to my advantage. But, if I'm to succeed, I can't hesitate.

I'm still under Owl Man's spell. I can't strike him or any of our allies. But Holy Moly, like all of the babies, is able to read my mind. I shoot a plea to it, letting it know that I'm in trouble, asking it to do something to Owl Man that will stop him from exerting his influence over me again.

Holy Moly's features darken when it sees what Owl Man has done to me. The babies take a very dim view of anyone who messes with their *mummy*. With a soft snarl, it throws itself at the much taller, pot-bellied figure, propelling itself like a white cannonball that has been shot into the air.

Owl Man tries to duck, but Holy Moly is too fast for him and attaches itself to his face. In a panic, he opens his mouth to roar a command at me, to tell me to call off the killer baby, but that's what I was banking on, and Holy Moly seizes the moment, doing exactly what I asked.

As Owl Man's lips part, the baby rams the vial between them, deep into his mouth. The end hits the back of his throat, then Holy Moly withdraws it and jams it in again, over and over, damaging the choking Owl Man's vocal cords.

As he makes incomprehensible noises and tries to shake the baby loose, Holy Moly pulls out the vial with one hand, then – balancing artfully on Owl Man's shoulder – sticks the fingers of its other hand into his mutilated mouth and rips its tiny claws around, slicing his tongue to shreds.

Holy Moly hops down with a giggle as Owl Man spits out pieces of blood-red flesh and moans. I'm sure the damage can be repaired, that his tongue and throat can be stitched back together. But it will take time. Right now he can't utter a single clear word.

Which means he can't tell me what to do.

Rage has released his grip on me, staring at the disabled Owl Man and considering his response. He doesn't react when I bend, slip free of his hold, and take the vial from a beaming Holy Moly. I stand and turn to face my old burly foe. He's studying me warily. I know I can't get the better of Rage in a fight, so I hold the vial out towards him.

'Your choice,' I snarl. 'But ask yourself this. Do you *really* want to be the one who kills off every human on the face of the planet?'

Rage stares at the vial, then glances over his shoulder at Dr Oystein, who is still grappling with Mr Dowling.

'Nuh-uh,' I grunt. 'You can't pass the buck. If you take this now and hand it to the doc, you'll be the one who decides the fate of billions of living, breathing people.'

'And if I don't take it?' Rage asks.

'Then the responsibility will be mine.'

Rage's eyes narrow. He thinks it over. Then he smiles. 'You know what? I used to think I was the biggest, baddest beast on the block. But you're more of a brute than I'll ever be.'

With that barbed compliment, he steps aside and crosses his arms, leaving the running of the show to me.

'One favour before I go,' I tell him.

Rage looks at me quizzically.

'Free me up to speak openly and fight.'

He bows like a loyal servant. 'I'm not sure if I need to repeat it, but I will, just to be safe. *The truth is in the eyes.* Now, I'm cancelling Owl Man's orders to say nothing about Dr Oystein's deception and not strike any of his troops. You've got the all-clear to say what you want and hit whoever you like.'

'Thanks, arsehole,' I grunt, and whack the side of Rage's head with the palm of my hand.

'Hey!' he yelps.

'Just checking,' I grin, then focus on a startled, bemused Carl Clay. 'You're a smart operator,' I say quickly. 'You should be able to recognise the truth. The doc lied to you. He wants to open this vial and kill off the last human survivors.'

'No,' Carl squeaks, shaking his head.

'Rage?' I snap.

'Like she said,' he sniffs.

'But ... that doesn't make sense ... he wouldn't ... he loves ...'

'He loves peace and quiet,' I growl. 'The trouble is humans aren't peaceful or quiet enough for him. He wants to replace them with the babies. For Dr

Oystein, the war has always been about getting hold of this –' I wave the vial of Schlesinger-10 at Carl '– and unleashing it on the world.'

Carl gulps. 'So what's your plan?' he wheezes. 'Do a runner with it?'

'Nah,' I grin. 'I've something better than that up my sleeve.'

My ribs are bound up tight. I pull a few of the bandages loose and jam the vial in nice and snugly. Then I slip behind Carl and wrap my arms round him.

'Jump,' I whisper. 'Carry me to where Dr Oystein and Mr Dowling are fighting. I'll take things from there.'

Carl looks back at me, then at Rage. Finally he stares at the spluttering Owl Man, who's reaching hopelessly towards us, trying to pull me back.

Carl makes up his mind and leaps. He uses all of the power in his frog-like legs to thrust us clear across the room, over the heads of the babies, mutants and Angels. We soar like birds above the mayhem. It's a weirdly calm moment. It reminds me of being in one of the Groove Tubes, the world fading out around me, safe, warm, hovering somewhere between the realms of reality and dreams.

Then we land next to the bloodied, wounded brothers. They're in bad shape and can barely stand. Their faces are a blood-drenched mess. One of Mr Dowling's eyes has popped out of its socket and dangles by its optic fibres on his cheek. A chunk of Dr Oystein's skull has been bitten off, exposing his brain. They're missing fingers. Their torsos have been carved open. But still they fight, ripping viciously at one another, unable to stop.

I thought I'd have to battle the doc, which is why I asked Rage to free me, but he's so preoccupied that he doesn't register my presence. In the end I don't even have to throw a punch, just reach into Dr Oystein's pocket, where he stuck the vial of Clements-13 earlier. It was crazy of him to bring it. But these are crazy times. I think the doc lost his mind a bit, being so close to the end. He couldn't think of anything except killing his brother, locating Holy Moly and securing the sample of Schlesinger-10. He screwed

up, and it's my job to make him pay for his mistake.

For a sickening moment my fingers don't find anything, and I think the doc fooled me, that he slyly disposed of the vial along the way. But then I strike hard glass and yank out the tube. I'm expecting Dr Oystein to scream and try to stop me, but he's too busy fighting with the ragged, savage clown.

I take a step away from the warring brothers. Mr Dowling is staring at me with his one good eye, shaking his head madly, gibbering like a monkey. He reaches towards me but is stopped by Dr Oystein, who carries on punching and kicking.

Master Zhang is almost upon us. He could probably break through the last of the mutants and babies and disable me. But instead he stops and looks at me with an unreadable expression.

Holding the vial firmly, I twist the rubber cork in the top, expecting it to resist. But, to my delight, it slips out smoothly. I turn the vial upside down and shake out the smaller vial nestled within. The cork of this one comes out easily too.

Then I'm down to the fragile glass tube. About ten

centimetres long, filled with the blood-red liquid that spells Armageddon for the living dead everywhere. I hold the tube above my head and gaze at it lovingly. Mr Dowling moans and throws himself at me, but Dr Oystein wrestles him to the floor. The doc doesn't seem to be aware of the threat. Maybe the hole in his skull has scrambled his senses. When I smash this tube open, every zombie on the face of the planet is doomed. He should be shrieking at me to stop. But all he can focus on is his brother.

I pause for a long, horrible second. I have a dark moment of doubt, when I consider the fact that I'm signing my own death warrant, when I don't think I'm brave enough to do this. For a terrible instant I feel like I'm going to chicken out.

Then I chuckle wryly.

'The hell with it. I've lived long enough.'

And I hurl the tube at the floor with all my might.

TWENTY -TWO

The glass container full of Clements-13 smashes upon contact. Strangely, that surprises me. I was expecting it to bounce. I knew that it *should* shatter, but the pessimist within me didn't think it *would*.

The red liquid splashes across the floor. No fumes rise from it. There are no crackling or hissing sounds. It's the same as if some paint had been spilled.

But everyone who sees it stops fighting. Those further back battle on, unaware of what's happened. Soldiers continue to fire their weapons. Mutants and babies pile forward. Screams echo through the air.

But those who saw the vial break know that something major has changed. The war has been decided. The battle for control of this planet has come to an abrupt end.

Mr Dowling and Dr Oystein stop clawing at one another. The clown staggers away from his brother, staring at the crimson liquid as it's absorbed by the dust on the floor. He reaches out, dabs a finger into the small pool, then touches it to his tongue, before falling on to his bum and sitting there, blinking like a confused child.

Dr Oystein pushes himself to his feet and sways drunkenly, fixated on the broken glass and the liquid. Then he looks at me.

'I'm sorry,' I croak. 'But I had to do it. You were wrong. The living must always be given another chance.'

Dr Oystein shakes his head slowly, awfully, and I feel wretched for the way I betrayed him, even though I had no choice.

'B . . .' Dr Oystein whispers, his voice gargly with blood.

'I hope you can forgive me,' I moan. 'We've got a week or two before it kills us. We can try to do good and help the living prepare for the takeover. I know you didn't want this, but there's no going back, so we might as well make the best of it, work together again one last time. Right?'

'B . . .' Dr Oystein repeats weakly.

And then he does something that strikes a cold stake through the space where my heart once nestled, fills me with dread and makes me suspect that all is not as done and dusted as I thought.

He smiles.

TWENTY
-THREE

Dr Oystein's smile is a thin, trembling thing, and it doesn't stay on his lips for long, yet it hits me harder than Dan-Dan ever did.

'Oh, B,' he sighs. 'I'm so sorry.'

'What the hell do *you* have to be sorry about?' I shout. I want him to be angry, to curse me, attack me, howl at the heavens while his senses dissolve.

Dr Oystein sits again and wipes blood from his face. He looks drained.

'I lied,' the doc says quietly. 'I fed you and the other Angels misinformation, knowing a day like this could come, hoping to trick you into doing my bidding. I was slyer than the offspring of a fox and a snake. I had to be.'

'What are you talking about?' I groan, looking to Master Zhang in case he can make any more sense. But he only shakes his head mutely and turns to Ingrid, who's still screaming and trying to pick ants from her eyes — they've burrowed through one eyeball and are hard at work on the other. Master Zhang studies her, decides she's too far gone to help, and drives his fingers through the side of her head, silencing her and releasing her from her agony.

'I mixed up the truth in all sorts of ways,' Dr Oystein says as Owl Man comes limping towards us, moaning painfully. 'I won't go through the list and correct every piece of erroneous information that I dangled in front of you. That would take too long. You can piece most of it together later, in your own time. It's enough to know this for now — although Albrecht was the more ingenious of us, I was always the master of the viruses.

'When I originally told you about Clements-13 and Schlesinger-10, I said that I had created both of them. That was true, except I created the zombie-destroying virus first, as I told you at our meeting earlier today. I said nothing of my breakthrough to Albrecht or Zachary, while I worked on manufacturing a virus which would be as lethal to humans as that one was to the undead.'

The fighting in the room begins to die down as word spreads of what has happened. The mutants and babies back away from the living and gather round Mr Dowling and Kinslow – Claudia is supporting him, as his leg seems to have been broken in the fighting when I wasn't paying attention – while the surviving humans regroup and move in closer, bewildered but respecting the ceasefire.

'When Albrecht found out what I'd done and what I was working on, he went wild and attacked me,' Dr Oystein continues. 'That's when I accidentally injected him with one of his mutant strains and sent him veering down the path of madness. Alone after that, but undeterred, I continued working on the human-killing virus. I was close to perfecting it when Zachary betrayed me.'

Dr Oystein smiles wanly at Owl Man, who has come to a standstill and is staring at me miserably.

'My nephew thought he was doing good,' Dr Oystein murmurs. 'He had not yet come to see that we needed to cleanse this planet of its human tyrants. He found out that a sample of Schlesinger-10 was still intact — I had kept it to run tests on. He didn't know where I had stored it, so he orchestrated attacks on all of my laboratories at the same time. Alas, I hadn't hidden the vial as cunningly as I thought. Zachary found it and delivered it to Albrecht.'

'Hold on,' I stop him. 'This doesn't make sense. You said you hadn't perfected the human-destroying virus yet.'

'That is correct,' Dr Oystein says calmly.

'So what did they steal?'

'The zombie-eradicating virus. They knew I would never dare release a virus targeted at humans as long as they had hold of its counterpart.'

'But ... no ... this is wrong,' I mutter. 'Mr Dowling had Schlesinger-10, the human-eliminating virus. He shared his thoughts with me. I know for definite that it was Schlesinger-10.'

'Yes,' Dr Oystein nods, and then he smiles that sickening smile again. 'That was my most cunning lie, the one for which I am most apologetic. When I learnt of Albrecht's fascination with you, I felt I could perhaps use you to retrieve the zombie-annihilating virus from him. But you would not have fetched it for me if you'd known what it really was. So, when I told you about the viruses, I switched names.

'Schlesinger-10 is the zombie-killing virus. Clements-13 is the human-killing virus. Not the other way round, as I pretended.'

My eyes bulge. 'But that means . . .'

'Yes,' Dr Oystein says sadly. 'When you took my vial of Clements-13 from me and smashed it open, you condemned humanity to extinction. You have done my job for me, and sentenced every living man, woman and child to an untimely end. That is why, even in my most triumphant moment, I am sorry — because I have turned you into an all-destructive god-dess of death.'

TWENTY
-FOUR

I'm reeling. I feel madness washing over me. In
desperation I look to the prince of chaos for hope.
'Is it true?' I scream at Mr Dowling inside my
head.

'*Yes,*' he answers miserably.

'But it can't be!' I roar out loud at Dr Oystein. 'If
that was the case, why lie to me when you captured
me at the pub and took me to your secret lab? You
thought I had the vial. Why bother with the charade
at that late stage?'

'Because I wanted you to do the foul deed for me,'

Dr Oystein says softly. 'I am a coward in many ways. I accept that I'm God's earthly agent, but I never asked for this much power. I wanted someone to lighten my load, to spare me the final, awful degradation.

'The plan was for Zachary to *accidentally* set you free of his control. Released from his influence, you would have wrestled the vial of Clements-13 from me and uncorked it in the belief that you were targeting the undead. If you'd failed, I would have opened it myself, but you were my first choice. I felt that if it was done by someone who thought they were doing good, perhaps God could forgive them.'

I stare at the deranged doctor. I don't want to believe what he's telling me, but I know it's true. His self-satisfied smile is all the proof that I need.

'I am genuinely sorry, B,' Dr Oystein says again. 'I would rather not have used you, but fate set things up this way. The Almighty knows I am a weak man. He chose one stronger than me to bear the dreadful burden.'

'Nice going, Becky,' Rage sneers, having trotted along behind Owl Man. 'With heroes like you, who needs villains?'

I can't respond. I'm numb with horror. I carry on staring at the doc, wanting this to be a bad dream or another of his lies.

'I've betrayed you,' Dr Oystein says, 'but it will be for the best in the long run. You must believe that. Humans *are* evil. This world *is* better off without the living. The babies will build a purer world. They'll care for its wildlife and flora. They won't overcrowd the continents or poison the atmosphere. They'll work to heal what has been wounded, and live in love and peace.

'And it will be under your guidance,' he says, addressing the stunned Angels. 'You'll be their guardians. You will help them grow and learn, teach them to be good, highlight the errors of the past, help them not to replicate the mistakes of their ancestors.

'If you wish, I can be part of that process. If you feel you have need of me, I will make myself available, although I am by no means essential. I have left instructions with numerous Angels across the globe. They will help you carry out my wishes and show you what needs to be done when your supplies of human brains run out.

'But, if you think that my sins are too grave, I'll accept execution too,' the doc finishes. 'To be honest, I would prefer it. This has been a hard life. I will be glad to step down from the path. If you choose to punish me, I won't resist.'

He smiles at me again, but warmly this time, offering me the right to pass judgement on him, to kill him if I wish.

'You lunatic!' someone screams behind us, shattering the strange solemnity of the moment. 'What the hell have you done?'

It's Vicky Wedge, lurching towards us, waving a handgun.

'I set the world free from your wicked grasp,' Dr Oystein retorts.

'You've killed us all!' Vicky shrieks.

'It was necessary,' Dr Oystein says.

'You have to stop it,' Josh thunders, striding up next to Vicky. His face is black with rage. 'There must be some way to counteract the virus. A cure. Don't make us force you to tell us.'

'There is no cure,' Dr Oystein says. 'Nothing can change what has been done. The virus is unleashed. It cannot be halted.'

'What if we cage ourselves in?' Josh shouts. 'Lock ourselves down and stop it from spreading?'

'Sacrifice yourselves to save the rest of the world?' Dr Oystein shakes his head. 'I admire your commitment, but this is a virus unlike any other that has ever wormed its way through our system. You can't contain it.'

My mind is whirring, but one thought has pushed its way to the fore. I know that fear will paralyse me if I don't act swiftly. So, trying not to think it through too much, I turn away from Dr Oystein and bend over. My body heaves as if I'm vomiting, and I clasp my hands to my chest as if in prayer.

'Poor girl,' Dr Oystein says. 'Nobody should have to go through what she has.'

'Forget about *her*,' Vicky Wedge screeches. 'Tell us how we stop this thing or I'll put a bullet through your head.'

'You would be doing me a great service if you did,' Dr Oystein answers icily. 'As I said, the virus cannot be stopped. Humanity is finished. A new age is upon us. There is nothing anybody can do to stop that now.'

'That's where you're wrong, doc,' I say, turning calmly.

While my back was turned, I slipped the vial of zombie-felling Schlesinger-10 out of its resting place in my bandages. While I was pretending to vomit and pray, I removed the cork on the first vial, turned it over, slid out the second vial, removed the cork on that, and let the ordinary glass tube slip into my hands.

I hold the tube of white liquid over my head so that everyone can see. As Dr Oystein's eyes fill with terror . . . as Owl Man tries to bark an order, but only produces a thick torrent of blood and shredded bits of tongue . . . as Master Zhang hurls himself at me, bellowing with a mixture of rage and fear . . . as everyone in the room focuses on me and the object in my hands . . .

I hurl the tube of Schlesinger-10 at the floor and watch with grim satisfaction as it fractures into hundreds of pieces and sends its deadly contents flying.

TWENTY
-FIVE

'What have you done?' Dr Oystein screams, mentally disintegrating in front of me, as I expected him to when I smashed open the first tube.

'Levelled the playing field,' I say evenly.

The doc gawps at me, jaw opening and shutting wordlessly.

Master Zhang bellows a curse in Chinese and propels himself towards me, chopping through the air in a blur, hell-bent on cracking my skull open. I stand firm, not only resigned but looking forward to the end.

Before Zhang can strike, Rage wrestles Vicky Wedge's gun from her, aims and fires. Our mentor's skull splinters and he collapses with a startled cry. He tries to rise, but Rage steps forward and fires three more bullets into his brain. Master Zhang is tough, but nobody is *that* tough. It's the end of the line for Dr Oystein's long-time friend and ally.

I nod at Rage, expecting him to finish me off next, but he only glares at me.

'This is insanity,' Dr Oystein whimpers. He's started to rock backwards and forwards. 'You've condemned us all.'

'Had to, doc,' I sniff. 'If people are truly evil, as you claim, then we're all in it together, the living, the undead and everyone between. It's not just one branch of humanity that deserves to be pruned — the whole bloody tree needs to come down.'

'But we were going to build anew!' Dr Oystein roars. 'We were going to put right what had gone wrong!'

'How?' I retort. 'By mimicking the Nazis and creating a super-race?'

The doc's face crumples. 'Is that how you see me?' he croaks.

'It's what you are,' I say quietly. 'You said you feel sorry for me. Well, I feel sorry for you too, because you became the thing you most hated. The Nazis broke and corrupted you, and turned you into one of their own in the process. It doesn't matter that your new race was a group of mutant babies instead of blond Aryans. You slaughtered billions of people in your quest to get rid of anyone who didn't fit in with your twisted vision.'

I turn slowly and point to Josh, Vicky Wedge and random other humans. 'Who are you, doc, to say they aren't worthy of life? Yeah, some are rotten to the core, but others are true and brave. It's not for the likes of you to pass sentence on them.'

'But they ruined this planet,' he whispers.

'Maybe,' I grimace. 'But they might have fixed it too. They messed up countless times, sure, but maybe they would have come good in the end.'

'No,' Dr Oystein says obstinately. 'My way was the only way forward.'

I shrug and point at the damp stains on the floor.

'Well, it's a pity if you're right, because that ain't gonna happen now.'

I lower my arm and address all of the people who are staring at me, their faces a mix of conflicting emotions. 'We're finished. You can bitch about it if you like, go on fighting, look for someone to blame. But there's no point. My advice is to seek out your loved ones and spend these last few days with them. If there's anything you ever dreamt of doing, this is the time to do it. You might want to spread the word, let other people know that we're doomed. Or maybe you'll decide they're better off not knowing. I'll leave that call to you.'

'*My beloved,*' Mr Dowling whispers inside my head. '*I am injured. I do not know if I will recover. Will you stay by my side and nurse me?*'

'No,' I tell him. 'I can't do that and, if you truly love me, you won't ask again. You have your babies for company.'

'*Our babies,*' he corrects me with a giggle.

'Yes — *our* babies.' I smile. 'Are they enough for you?'

He considers it, then makes a gurgly noise and whines aloud, 'Yes.'

'Then I'll leave you in their care,' I mutter, blowing him a kiss. 'With one exception, if you don't mind. Holy Moly?' The baby looks at me expectantly. It doesn't seem to have absorbed the consequences of the unfolding drama. I don't think any of the babies understand what has happened. 'Will you guide me to the surface?'

'*of course, mummy,*' Holy Moly says happily. '*i love you, mummy.*'

'*we love you, mummy,*' the other babies echo.

'I love you guys too, creepy and lethal as you are,' I chuckle.

Then I turn away from everyone, Dr Oystein, Mr Dowling, the last of the Angels, the mutants, the humans, Owl Man, my enemies and friends. I'm sure we could bat this back and forth all night, levelling accusations and dishing out blame, but, really, what's left that's worth saying?

Picking up the baby with the hole in its skull, I head for the world above. And despite those who call out to me, who ask me to stop and tell them more about the viruses, and what led us to this point, and if there's any way to reset the clocks and avert the catastrophe, I never pause or look back. There's no reason why I should. I mean, why waste precious time on a load of walking dead folk?

TWENTY -SIX

A couple of minutes later, as I'm shuffling through the tunnels, someone rushes up behind me. I stop and wait, staring ahead at nothing, hoping it's a furious soldier or mutant come to cut me down.

No such luck.

'You really screwed us all back there,' Rage chuckles.

'What do you want?' I ask wearily.

'Thought I'd tag along,' he says cheerfully. 'The war room's like a funeral parlour. I don't know how long it's gonna take that lot to recover. Maybe they won't. Maybe they'll just stand around moping until they drop.'

I turn slowly. There are no lights in this stretch of corridor, but I can make out Rage by the glow from Holy Moly's eyes, which switched to red when it sensed a possible threat. 'You seem to be taking this in your stride,' I note archly.

Rage shrugs. 'Nothing I can do about it now. If I'd known what you were up to, I'd have stopped you, but it's too late, so I might as well go with the flow.' He hesitates. 'In fact, I'm not sure I *would* have stopped you, even if I could.'

'Pull the other one,' I snort.

'I'm serious,' he says. 'This is a rotten world. I used to think that didn't bother me. I dealt with it by being rotten myself. But the doc made me believe that we could be more than scum. I let myself hope. When I realised I'd been an idiot, that the world was as viciously ridiculous as I'd always thought, it hurt. I tried behaving the way I did before. Hell, I tried to be even nastier. But I don't know if I could have gone on that way. It's hard to revel in the dark when you've caught a glimpse of the light.'

I cock my head curiously. 'Imminent death has brought out the poet in you.'

Rage laughs. 'Yeah. Isn't that a tragic joke?'

I turn and limp on through the darkness, Rage just behind. We don't say anything else as we creep through the tunnels, avoiding the battle between the soldiers, mutants and zombies which is still raging in the cavern. Holy Moly senses my glum mood and is silent too.

I'm not sure how long we wind through the sub-terranean corridors, but eventually we hit railway tracks and make our way to the Tube station at Tower Hill, further west than I imagined. We join the reviveds who are thronging towards the surface. It must be night up top. They're setting off in search of prey, no idea that last orders are just a couple of weeks away.

Emerging out of the gloom, we cross the road and sit looking down on the famous old Tower of London. I think about the Beefeater who was guarding the entrance the last time I went in. I smile as I wonder if he's still at his post. Even if he is, he won't be manning it now — he'll have set off on the prowl with the rest of his kind, in search of brains. But, if I'm still here in the morning, I'll have a look before I move on. For old times' sake.

'I wonder what Dr Oystein and the others are doing down there now?' Rage muses aloud. 'They might turn on each other and finish off the job, rather than wait for the virus to take them. I bet the doc's gone loop-the-loop. Maybe he's bashed his head open on the floor, all that hard work and planning undone in a couple of seconds by a brutish, ignorant girl. No offence intended.'

'Get stuffed,' I sniff.

Rage laughs and I smile. I don't mind his teasing. In a way it's reassuring. It's nice to know that at least some things haven't changed.

Rage pretends to yawn. Then he hops to his feet and punches the air a few times, like a boxer warming up. 'Right,' he says brightly. 'I'm off.'

'Where?' I ask.

'Don't know. I'll see where the night leads me. Going to squeeze in a few adventures before the end, live the high life as much as I can. This could be an interesting fortnight.'

'Want me to come with you?'

'Hardly,' he growls. 'I don't want to be seen with the girl who ended life on Earth as we know it. What would that do for my reputation?'

'Drop dead,' I snap.

'Thanks to your little trick with the vial, that's the one thing you can be sure of,' he grimaces.

And then, without a word of goodbye or a wave, he sets off, whistling jauntily, to round a corner and slip out of sight, never to be seen or heard from again.

TWENTY -SEVEN

I sit where I am for a long time, bouncing Holy Moly on my knee, too weary to push on. I won't stay here forever. I'll get my arse in gear sooner or later. Just not yet.

I don't have much time left to play with, so I give careful consideration to what I want to do with it. I'll go to the Bow Quarter first, tell Ciara what Reilly said, let the twins know that the writing's on the wall.

After that, I'll drop by County Hall and free Mr Burke if he's still there. He's only a brain-dead zombie, I know, but I don't like the thought of him being caged up for these last few days, perishing alone and hungry in a prison cell. I'll rest easier if I let the poor bugger roam free.

When I've seen to those obligations, I'll head for New Kirkham. I'm in bad shape so I don't know if I can make it that far. But, if I can, I'll share the news with Jakob and his crew, give them a chance to prepare for the end and say their farewells. I liked it there. The town was a symbol of hope. It will be nice to see Biddy Barry and her people again, though I'm not sure how they'll react when I tell them what I did underground. Maybe they'll string me up and chuck spears at my head, finish me off before the virus can.

Assuming the residents of New Kirkham don't kill me, I'll try to crawl back to County Hall and head for the Groove Tubes. Fill one of them if they're not already topped up, slip in and bliss out. That way, when the world ends, I won't even know. Fade away with a sleepy smile on my face, without having to suffer through the human race's death throes.

I make a sad moaning sound and Holy Moly looks

at me, concerned. *'are you all right, mummy?'* the baby asks.

'Not really,' I sigh. 'But I'll be OK as long as you stick with me. You won't leave me, will you?'

'no,' the baby beams. *'i love you, mummy. i'll never leave you alone.'*

I hug Holy Moly and kiss the top of its head. The baby giggles, delighted with itself, and snuggles up to me, safe, warm, happy. It doesn't care that the world is ending. It's with its mummy and that's all that matters.

I think about all that has happened, the fighting, the lies, the deaths, the Apocalypse we've brought upon ourselves.

I don't regret uncorking the zombie-destroying virus. I wasn't about to hand control of this world to Dr Oystein. You can never let the bad guys win, even if they've taken all the other options away.

Maybe there was another way. By eliminating the zombies and mutants, I removed any hope our race had of getting back on its feet. Maybe the Angels wouldn't have harvested the human babies as Dr

Oystein planned. Maybe they'd have hatched the embryos when it was safe and set free a new generation of living kids.

But, even if some of them had bucked the doc's wishes, others would have tried to push ahead with his blueprint. The war would have continued. The same old story, people – alive or undead – taking sides, battling on, killing and destroying.

This isn't the end of the world, merely the end of our part in it. Life on Earth will continue. Animals will thrive. Maybe a new intelligent species will emerge, inspired by God or simple evolutionary forces, to plug the gap we've left behind.

Or maybe nature won't tinker with the curse of intelligence again. Maybe one set of destructive overlords was enough. The forces that control these things didn't bring back the dinosaurs when their reign ended. There's no reason to think they'll bring back humanity either.

Whatever happens, in many ways I truly believe that the planet is well rid of us. Dr Oystein was mad, but a lot of what he said made sense. We've done so much damage to ourselves and this poor world. Some of us stood up for what was right, but most of us kept our heads low and let things go down the pan, happy to wash our hands of the mess as long as we weren't directly involved.

Like the way I put up with Dad's racism and bullying. I should have challenged him every day, every time he said something cruel or raised a hand to Mum or me. Every one of us with a conscience needed to stand up and shout out, not just at occasional rallies, not just by casting our votes in elections, but all the time.

We moaned about crooked politicians, but how many of us stood up to the back-stabbing bastards? We complained about bankers, property developers and soulless huge companies, but we gave them our money, didn't we?

We were happy with our TVs, computers and smartphones, our designer gear, fast food and cheap travel. We tutted when we heard that a species was on the verge of extinction, rolled our eyes when our leaders exploited poor sods in other countries. But, as long as things were sweet on the home front, most of us were content to go along for the ride.

We didn't look to the future. We lived for the moment, squeezing the planet dry, selfish sons (and daughters — I'm far from blameless) of bitches, not worrying about what we were leaving behind for the next generations. We . . .

Oh, to hell with it. I don't want to sit here whining. There's no point trying to list all the ways we went wrong, all the things we could and should have done. It's easy to be wise after the fact. We screwed up royally and got what we had coming — it's as simple as that.

I'll dawdle here a while longer, gather what little strength I have left, then move on with Holy Moly to try and complete my list of errands before I hit my expiry date. The time for speeches has come and gone. Besides, I'm a pariah, not a prophet. It's a bit rich, the girl who brought down the world, trying to figure out how that it could have been saved.

With a shaky groan, I struggle to my feet and let Holy Moly slip to the ground. I run a hand over the nails sticking out of my head and chuckle. Enough of the meek and mild crap. If I have to go – and I have to – I'm going in style. No more sitting around and moping. When I bow out, it will be with fire in my belly and a lip-twisting grin.

'I'm B Smith!' I yell at the sky, making a fist and shaking it above my head to show my defiance. 'Within a couple of weeks, every man, woman, child, zombie and mutant on the face of this planet will be dead and gone. And good bloody riddance to the lot of us!'

Then I pick up Holy Moly, laugh with savage delight, and shuffle off into the darkness of the ever-lasting night.

LATER . . .

A

The fabled white light. So many people spoke of it over the years. The light at the end of the tunnel, beckoning on the dead, guiding souls towards their final resting place. I thought it was a myth, but it's ahead of me now, warm and bright, welcoming me home. I smile and reach towards it.

'No,' someone says, pushing my arms down. 'Stay still a while longer, please. I haven't finished mopping up the liquid.'

I think about that, frowning. It's a strange thing for a celestial being to say.

Then, as my senses start to swim back into place, I become aware of a towel draped over my head, a sponge being dabbed around the inside of my stomach. The light isn't a heavenly, other-worldly ball. It's the glow of a bulb.

I try pushing myself away and shouting, but my mouth is full of overgrown teeth. I can only moan.

'Easy,' the voice comes again. 'You have nothing to fear. I'm looking after you.'

I want to ask who it is and what's happening, but I can't produce any words. Since I'm in a helpless position, I relax and let the person go about their business. Memories return and it doesn't take me long to realise where I am and what must be going on.

I told the twins and Ciara the bad news, and what I was planning next. They were distraught, but the twins hid from their gloom as best they could by promising to go and release Mr Burke, saving me some time. They were going to search for Dr Oystein after that, to help him any way they could if he was still alive. Their love for him hadn't diminished, regardless of what he'd done.

Ciara stayed in the Bow Quarter and said she'd keep things ticking over in case any of the Angels returned. Loyal to the end. She held herself together while we were there, but I'm sure she wept bitterly for Reilly when we left.

After a long, hard trek, I made it to New Kirkham and told Jakob about the Dowling brothers, the viruses, how things had played out. He thanked me for delivering the news, promised to inform the others in the settlement, but advised me to get the hell out of there before he did.

'They'll hate you,' he said sadly. 'And me, for my assocation with you. They might even kill me for being the bearer of the message, but there's no reason for you to be killed too.'

I begged Jakob to come with me, but he wouldn't budge. He regarded the citizens of New Kirkham as his people now and he was determined to see out his days there, even if the reward for his loyalty was execution. He wished me well, told me not to blame myself, and helped slip me out.

The journey back to London was an agonising

nightmare. I could barely walk more than a few steps without having to stop and recuperate. I'll never know how I made it — sheer stubbornness, I suppose. Must have taken me three or four days.

But finally I staggered back into County Hall. It had been ransacked and badly burnt in places by Mr Dowling's mutants, but luckily for me they hadn't touched the Groove Tubes. They were empty, so I filled one, undressed, blew a farewell kiss to the world and clambered in.

That should have been the end of matters, but someone must have found me and dragged me out, either because they thought I needed help or because they wanted me to be around for the pain and hurt. Looks like I won't be skipping the end of the world after all.

I try not to feel too much resentment as the person tending me swabs out my nostrils and ear canals with cotton buds. I probably didn't deserve an easy exit, not after all I'd done. It's apt that I was hauled out to bear witness to the destruction. I won't complain or ask to be returned to the Tube. As the old saying goes, it's a fair cop.

'Tilt your head back and open your mouth wide,' the person says. My ears must still be partly blocked because I can't make out if it's a man or a woman.

Whoever it is, he or she slides a drill up under the towel and sets to work on my teeth, first removing the remains of the false ones that Mr Dowling installed, then focusing on my oversized fangs. I'm amazed they've sprouted as much as they have. I can only have been in the Groove Tube a few days. Maybe the doc found a way to strengthen the solution since I last went for a refreshing dip.

The drilling goes on for ages. The person works carefully, like a dentist, stopping every few minutes to let my teeth cool down. When we're getting close to the end, he or she sets the drill aside and finishes the job with a sturdy metal file.

I try to say something, but nothing comes out.

'Wait,' I'm told. 'The device in your throat needs to be replaced.'

A hand sneaks up inside me, through the gap where my lungs should be, and fiddles with the little pumping mechanism on the inner wall of my throat, which Mr Dowling had inserted. The person talks while fitting me with a new speech box.

'You're lucky that your stomach wall was cut away. It makes cleaning out the liquid a much simpler task. No need for an enema this time.'

I chuckle mutely, thanking Heaven for small mercies.

There's a bit more tinkering, then the person steps back and says, 'Try that.'

'What do you want me to say?' I ask.

'Amazing! So clear, after all this time.'

'After all *what* time?' I grumble, trying to take off the towel so that I can get a good look at whoever I'm talking to.

'Easy.' The person stops me. 'We'll be able to operate on your eyes, but not for a while. In the mean time I have a thick pair of sunglasses for you, made with prescription lenses. They're more like goggles, but trust me, you'll need them.'

I wait impatiently until the glasses are fetched and set in place. I try to get up, but my toebones have lengthened and I almost topple over. 'Sorry,' the person says. 'Let me chop those off for you. I'll do your fingerbones too.'

As my personal attendant is working on the bones, I tug the towel off my head and wince as light floods in. The glasses are incredibly thick, and the room has been subtly lit, but, even so, at first it's like staring straight into the sun.

'I did warn you,' my helper says as I cover my eyes with an arm.

'Yeah, yeah,' I snap. 'Everyone's an expert. Why don't you . . .'

I stop. I've caught sight of my fingerbones. They've regrown in the Tube, but are far longer than they ever were before, at least sixty or seventy centimetres. The toebones that haven't been trimmed yet are a similar length.

'How the hell did they grow so much?' I gasp. 'What did the doc add to the solution?'

'Nothing,' comes the reply. 'It's the same as it always was.'

'But my teeth and bones never grew like this before,' I note.

'That's because you were never in the Tube as long as you were this time.'

'What are you talking about?' I frown. 'It can't have been more than a few days, a week at most, otherwise there wouldn't be anyone around to pull me out. Unless . . .'

Hope flares within me.

'Did the viruses fail?' I shout.

'No,' the person says quietly. 'Clements-13 and Schlesinger-10 did what they were designed to do. Every human, zombie and mutant perished.'

'But then how . . . who . . .?'

'I'll explain it all shortly. But I think you should shower first, after I've dealt with the rest of these bones. Then we will dress you. And then –'

'Sod that,' I growl, forcing myself to my feet. It takes me a few seconds to find my balance, but then I steady myself and look around.

At first the room is a ball of blinding light and my head fills with pain. But I hang tough and, gradually, the light starts to dim and objects swim into focus. I see the Groove Tube, the towel on the floor, my severed toebones. I turn and there are the walls and door, the windows covered with thick curtains to block any outside light.

Then I turn towards the person who fished me out. The first thing I realise is that he or she is about my height and totally naked. The next thing I notice is that it's *not* a he or she — this individual has no genitals. There's just smooth flesh where the legs meet.

Stunned, my gaze shoots up. He ... she ... *it* is smiling shyly. Its hair is a dark brown colour, cut tight to the scalp. I don't recognise the face. What I do recognise, however, are the pure white eyes and the hole in its scalp.

'*Holy Moly?*' I wheeze.

The smile widens. My rescuer nods with delight. And says, 'Hello, Mummy. It's good to have you back.'

B

I let the adult Holy Moly shower me, saying nothing as I'm gently rinsed down, all the gunk washed away.

'Your ears have rusted,' Holy Moly tuts. 'They'll need to be replaced. It will be a simple task, but you'll have to put up with these for the time being. I don't think the rust will affect your hearing.

'We'll fix your stomach too,' Holy Moly says as it hoses out my hollow insides. 'Not in the ugly way that Daddy stitched bits of flesh together. We'll clone your flesh and create a covering that looks almost the way it did before it was sliced open.'

Turning off the shower, Holy Moly pats me dry and wraps me in a purple robe. In a daze I sit, and the one-time eerie baby hums as it focuses on the bones sticking out of my fingers and toes. It sheared off the remainder of them before putting me in the shower, but now it vigorously files down the stumps, reducing them and smoothing them out.

'How?' I finally wheeze as Holy Moly is working on my left hand, having finished with both feet and the fingers of my right hand.

'You'll have to be more precise than that, Mummy,' Holy Moly says without pausing.

'How are you here?' I ask. 'How am *I* here? Why aren't we dead like all the others?'

Holy Moly nods happily, as if that was the question it had anticipated. 'All of the babies survived. We were resistant to the viruses.'

'Mr Dowling found a way to counteract the viruses?' I croak.

'Only in our case,' Holy Moly says. 'Since we were laboratory-grown clones, he was able to tinker with our DNA. He couldn't be certain that we'd survive, but he was quietly optimistic.'

'He never said,' I mumble.

'He never told anyone.' Holy Moly giggles. 'At the time we couldn't understand why we were the only ones who didn't drop dead. It was decades before we figured it out.'

'*Decades?*' I say weakly.

'As for Mummy,' Holy Moly beams, 'you were saved by the Groove Tube. You were dying when you entered, but the liquid nourished you and slowed down the rate of decay. If the virus had been active for longer, you would have eventually perished, but it only had a lifespan of several years. Once it passed from your system, the liquid began to restore all of the cells that had been destroyed, and you have been kept in a nice, neutral state throughout the centuries since.'

'*Centuries?*' I cry.

'Dr Oystein didn't know that a zombie could ride out the effects of the viruses inside a Groove Tube,' Holy Moly goes on. 'If he had, he would have made more and retreated to them with his Angels. They all could have been saved.'

'Are you saying that I'm the only one who survived?' I ask shakily.

Holy Moly purses its lips. 'Actually there were several others, scattered across the world. They had either been recovering in Groove Tubes when the virus was unleashed, or sought the refuge of them like you, so as not to have to face the end of civilisation.

'Unfortunately we didn't discover them until after we'd begun to travel. We didn't leave this country for two hundred and sixteen years. By the time we found others like you, the Tubes maintaining them had malfunctioned. They died like foetuses in their wombs. We buried them. We thought you would like that.'

I'm still wearing the glasses. I lift them now, even though it pains me, to stare at Holy Moly directly as I ask, 'How long was I in there?'

Holy Moly answers casually. 'Nine hundred and ninety-nine years, three hundred and fifty-seven days exactly.'

There's a long, stunned silence. Then I slowly replace my glasses.

'Almost a thousand years,' I say hoarsely.

'Tomorrow will mark the anniversary of when you released the viruses,' Holy Moly confirms. 'That's why I fished you out today. We wanted you to be with us to celebrate the millennium.'

'A thousand years,' I whisper. 'I must be dreaming.'

'Silly Mummy,' Holy Moly laughs. 'You know zombies can live for thousands of years. In fact, we think you might live even longer than Dr Oystein anticipated, having spent so long in a Groove Tube. We can't be certain, but we're keeping our fingers crossed.'

I start to tremble. Holy Moly shoots me a sympathetic look, then hugs me.

'*it's ok, mummy,*' it whispers, sounding like it used to when it was a baby, a thousand years ago. '*we'll take care of you. we love our mummy.*'

'What's it like out there?' I moan. 'Did you create the paradise that Dr Oystein hoped you would? Did you find the embryos and bring back the human race? Is war a thing of the past or are things worse than ever?'

'There's only one way to find out,' Holy Moly smiles, offering me its hand.

I stare at the hand, then up into Holy Moly's face. 'Why wait so long?' I ask. 'Why not fish me out before this?'

'We had to grow first,' Holy Moly says. 'We didn't want to remove you until we were sure we knew what we were doing. Then we decided to establish ourselves, explore the world and lay the foundations of our new society, so that you'd have something nice to emerge to. By the time we were ready, it was so close to the thousand-year anniversary that we figured we might as well wait, to make it more special.

'The others will be so excited to see you,' it continues. 'I've been your attendant for most of your time here. A few more helped, and we've allowed a trickle of others to visit, but most of our kind have never seen you, apart from those who were alive when the viruses were released.'

'You mean you've cloned more of yourselves since then?'

'Oh yes,' Holy Moly says. 'There are a lot more of us now.'

'How many?' I ask.

Holy Moly smiles and twitches its fingers. 'Come and find out.'

I gaze through the door of the laboratory into the old courtyard at County Hall, reluctant to leave my cocoon, wanting to learn more about this strange new world before I take my place in it.

'Not the courtyard, Mummy,' Holy Moly says, having read my mind the way it could when it was an infant. 'We're not in County Hall. The Thames flooded a long time ago. Most of London is under water now. We moved you to a safe location before that happened.'

'Where?' I ask.

Holy Moly smiles and twitches its fingers again.

'OK,' I snap, getting to my feet. 'You don't need to force me. I never backed away from a challenge in the past, and I'm not about to start now.'

'Now *there* is the Mummy that I know and love,' Holy Moly chuckles. 'The bitch is back.'

I cock my head at Holy Moly, wondering if that was meant as an insult or a compliment. When I see that it's the latter, I nod with satisfaction. 'Damn right,' I mutter. 'And she's ready to roll.'

Then, not giving myself any time to feel butterflies in my stomach — not that I even have a stomach at the moment — I ignore Holy Moly's hand, shoot the naked neuter a tight smile, then march to the door, kick it open and step out into the future, to see what it has in store for me.

The beginning ...

ZOM-B was written between
7th April 2008 and 5th November 2014

GRAB

DARREN SHAN
ZOM-B

DARREN SHAN
**ZOM-B
UNDERGROUND**

DARREN SHAN
**ZOM-B
CITY**

DARREN SHAN
**ZOM-B
ANGELS**

DARREN SHAN
**ZOM-B
BABY**

DARREN SHAN
**ZOM-B
GLADIATOR**

#HASHTAGREADS

Bringing the best YA your way

TOMMY WALLACH

MORGAN MATSON

ROBYN SCHNEIDER

CASSANDRA CLARE

CLARE FURNISS

DARREN SHAN

HONOR & PERDITA CARGILL

C.J. FLOOD

SOPHIE MCKENZIE

STEPHEN CHBOSKY

AMY ALWARD

JENN BENNETT

#R

PAIGE TOON

GAYLE FORMAN

BECCA FITZPATRICK

SCOTT WESTERFELD

S.J. KINCAID

Join us at **HashtagReads**,
home to your favourite YA authors

Follow us on Twitter
@HashtagReads

Find us on Facebook
HashtagReads

Join us on Tumblr
HashtagReads.tumblr.com